Trespass

PIERCEHAVEN BOOK 3

ROBIN MERRILL

New Creation Publishing

New Creation Publishing
Madison, Maine

For Brandon, Alana,
and your awesome family.
I adore you.

Chapter 1

Emily knocked on James's front door. His truck was in the driveway, so she knew he was home. She was about to abandon etiquette and just turn the knob herself when he opened the door.

"Hi." He didn't sound excited to see her. That had been happening a lot lately. She slapped that unpalatable thought out of her mind.

"Hi, yourself. You look nice." She wasn't being entirely ironic. He didn't look nice *exactly*, with his filthy jeans, rubber boots, and sweatshirt with the sleeves cut off. His hair stood straight up in the air, and he looked exhausted. Yet, the appearance made her stomach do a backflip, so in truth, he did look fantastic—to her anyway.

He didn't appear to take the compliment well, so she stepped inside and wrapped her arms around his neck, standing on her tiptoes to kiss him on the cheek. He smelled scrumptious; sure, there was the faint remnant of eau de bait, but it was overpowered by the clean, sharp smell of fresh ocean air. She could practically smell the wind in his hair.

He pulled away from her slowly, but more quickly than she wanted him to and certainly more quickly than he had been doing in the recent past.

"You OK?" she asked.

"Yeah," he said, not looking at her. "I just got in from hauling. Was about to jump in the shower."

So he was annoyed that she'd interrupted that. He didn't say it. But he said it just the same.

"Sorry," she said.

"It's OK. You need anything right now, or do you mind if I go clean up?"

"Go ahead," she said quickly. "I'll just Netflix."

"All right, but no *Battlestar Galactica* without me." He smirked and headed toward the bathroom.

She turned and surveyed the living room before collapsing on the couch. James had relaxed tremendously on his "no women allowed in his house without a chaperone" rule since they'd become officially engaged. She was grateful for that. She grabbed the remote and put her feet up, smiling at his Galactica comment. She'd already watched the series at least five times, but this was his first trip through, and she was immensely enjoying watching it anew through his eyes. He'd sworn he wouldn't like it—"Don't do sci-fi," he'd said, but he'd changed his mind after only a few episodes. She'd been right. Of course.

She started an episode of *Psych* and then stared at the screen blankly as she thought about all the stuff they still had to do—and soon. She didn't want to be one-of-those-brides, was committed to not being obnoxious about the whole thing, but it seemed James was trying to push her off the bridezilla cliff. She was still mentally ticking off her to-do list when he reappeared, with dirt, salt, and fishing scents washed off him. He still looked fantastic, of course, but somehow a little less spicy.

"Hungry?" He sat down beside her and put a hand on her knee.

She wasn't hungry, had been nervous-snacking all day, but she said, "Sure." She'd actually committed to losing a few pounds before the big day, but making that commitment had only made her crave salt and sugar all the more.

"Want to have a pizza delivered?" His chest vibrated with a silent laugh.

She got the joke, but she didn't laugh. There was most certainly no pizza delivery on the island, so "have it delivered" meant he was asking her to go pick it up. "Sure," she said again. Pizza. Just what the diet ordered. "You call it in. And you're buying." She vowed to only eat one piece, but even as she made the vow, she knew she'd break it. He got up to go to the phone, and she listened to him make the order, enjoying the sound of his voice. She couldn't believe how utterly in love with this man she was.

"Twenty minutes," he said, returning to the couch. "So, how are you enjoying your summer vaca, Teach?"

"I won't lie and say it's not wonderful. I'm enjoying sleeping as late as I want. But I do miss the kids." She paused. "Can we talk about the wedding?" She looked at him closely to see if he was annoyed, but he didn't flinch.

"Sure," he said, "what do you want to talk about?"

"We really need to get the invitations sent out. So I still need your list."

He rolled his neck as if to get the kinks out. "I thought I was just going to do word of mouth. I don't really care who shows up."

She tried to keep her voice level. "We can't afford to feed the whole island." She tried to keep the pleading out of her voice, but she was feeling desperate.

He finally looked at her. "Fine. I will get you a list."

She was not comforted, however, as this was not the first time he had promised a list.

"What else?" he asked.

"I need to know where my people are going to sleep."

Now he looked annoyed. "We've discussed this, haven't we? We'll find places for them. Islanders are hospitable. I don't want to start asking people to host before we even know who's coming—"

"We're not going to get RSVPs until we send out invitations," she interrupted, "and I want to be able to assure people they'll have a bed when I invite them." She paused for a few seconds, but then more words spilled through the gate. "My sister is not comfortable being told she will just be put up somewhere. She wants to know ahead of time where she'll be sleeping, and I don't blame her."

As if he didn't even hear what she had just said, he said, "Things just have a way of working out on the island. You know that. Don't sweat it."

She took a deep breath. "I do know that. But can you just help me out here if for no other reason than to ease my anxiety?"

"OK, so make a list of who you think will come for sure, and then call people and ask them how many people they can host. Then match them up on your guest list."

This was not the first time they had had this conversation, yet they seemed to have made no progress. "James, I don't want to call people I hardly know and ask them to lend my sister a bed. That's why I had asked you to do it. Can you please call them? They're your friends."

He folded his arms across his chest. "OK, I'll call them. Just give me the list."

"I already did," she said and this time she failed to stop herself from snapping.

He looked at her sharply. "You do know this is fishing season? I've been a little busy."

Of *course* she knew it was fishing season, but he couldn't blame all his busyness on the lobsters. On most nights, he came home from hauling traps and then went straight to basketball practice. She didn't want to resent basketball or his players, but she had thought basketball was a *winter* sport. She hadn't realized he'd be coaching nearly every day all summer long. Apparently, on Piercehaven, basketball was a summer sport as well. And a fall sport. And spring. And if there were a fifth season, they would play basketball then too.

She took a deep breath. "I do know that you're busy. But I really need your help on this."

"Well, I think I've *misplaced* your list," he said with attitude. He paused and then said without looking at her, "You should go get the pizza. It's going to get cold."

Chapter 2

Emily cried all the way to The Pizza Place. She couldn't help but think that maybe James didn't want to marry her at all. He certainly wasn't very excited about the wedding. She had ten other things to talk to him about, but now she was scared to bring anything up, which meant she would put it off till the next time she saw him, which meant pushing back the planning even further. It was late June. The wedding was August 5. She didn't have much time to push anything anywhere.

To make matters worse, the woman who handed her the pizza was the mom of one of her students. "Hi, Miss Morse!" she said brightly.

"Hi, Kim. Please, call me Emily. I didn't know you worked here." She handed her James's debit card.

"Just started." She slid the Visa through the card reader with extra force.

Emily knew that Kim's husband was a lobsterman, and therefore the family probably didn't need a second income. At least, a lot of lobstermen's wives didn't work outside the home. "Well, congratulations then."

She snorted. "I don't think it's congratulation-worthy. My parents own the joint. Caleb and I have just moved in upstairs."

Oh. Caleb and her. Not hubby.

"How are the wedding plans coming?" Kim asked, in an obvious maneuver to move the small talk away from her own life.

Emily was able to forestall the tears, but she didn't manage to prevent the stress from appearing on her face. She hurried to try to cover it. "Thank you so much for asking. It's coming along fine. I'm just a little overwhelmed."

Kim nodded understandingly. "Is anyone helping you?"

It was only four words, but there was a load of knowledge packed within them. Emily knew that somehow Kim knew James wasn't fully on board with the planning process. Emily punched in James's pin number and tried to keep the tears out of her voice. "Not really."

Kim gave her hand a quick pat. "Well, you need to ask for help then. Don't expect a man to do it. Especially a man during fishing season. Where are you having the wedding?"

At first, Emily ignored her question, focusing on the comment she had made just prior to it. "We're both getting married, so shouldn't he help with the planning? He should have some say in how this thing goes."

"I don't know James that well, but I can guarantee he does not care about wedding details. You plan your perfect day, and then you hand him the bill. Unless your parents are paying for it?" She raised both eyebrows and turned her head to the side; Emily had learned that this expression meant an islander knew they were being nosey, but that they were allowed to be nosey because they were an islander.

"My parents have offered no such thing, and I have not asked. I shouldn't need to. We aren't planning on anything expensive or elaborate."

"Are you getting married in your basement church?"

Emily laughed. "No, I don't think we'd fit, and I don't think Abe would love for that to happen. Although he would probably let us if we asked."

"It must be a pretty big basement. I hear a lot of people talking about going to church there these days."

"It's pretty full on Sunday mornings. That's for sure. We are going to have the wedding at Pig Poop Point."

Kim laughed suddenly and loudly, making Emily's cheeks hot. "Why would you get married way out there?"

"It's just so beautiful," Emily said, but she knew it was more than that. The language lover within her also really loved the name. How many people could say they got married at Pig Poop Point? The alliteration made her quiver with excitement.

"True," Kim said slowly. "But there are a lot of beautiful spots on this island. And I don't know where people would park for a Pig Poop wedding. And it's so rocky out there. Are you inviting old people? I'd be worried about them slipping and tripping on the rocks."

"Are you a wedding planner? Because maybe you should be." Emily laughed nervously. "These are the things I need to work out. But I'm not sure where to start."

"Well, I'm no wedding planner, but I'm happy to help. I like social things."

This was music to Emily's weary ears. She didn't know Kim, at all, but she did know that she did *not* like social things. "Won't Caleb be embarrassed if you spend the summer helping with his teacher's wedding?"

"Whether or not Caleb is embarrassed about something is pretty far down on my list of things to worry about." Her face grew brighter as she spoke. She looked genuinely excited. Emily wondered if she was an angel. A wedding-planning angel sent by God.

"You're serious?" It seemed too good to be true.

"I am. Are you having it catered?"

"I don't know. James wants it to be a potluck, but I'm not sure I want to do that. I don't want to ask people to bring food to my wedding, especially when all of my people are coming from the mainland. They're not going to be able to cook when they get here. Should I really make them bring potato salad on the ferry? That's not fair." She realized she was babbling, and cut herself off.

"Oh dear," Kim said. "You really are stressed out. Take your pizza home. Then come back here. Either tonight or tomorrow. Or whenever. I'm here most of the time now, and only busy around suppertime. Come back, and then we'll sit down and make a plan. I'll be happy to help."

Emily couldn't believe her ears. Why hadn't she consulted with this woman two months ago? "I don't know how I'll ever thank you."

"Guarantee Caleb straight A's for the rest of his English classes."

Emily cringed.

"Just kidding. Now get that pizza back to your man." She winked.

Emily decided then that she really liked Caleb's mom.

When she got back to James's house, she didn't tell him about her new wedding planner, but she did ask about Kim's husband. "How well do you know Caleb Aronson's dad?"

James shrugged. "Pretty well, why?"

"I just ran into Caleb's mom at The Pizza Place. She's working there now, and she said that she and Caleb had moved into the apartment above the restaurant—"

"I didn't know there *was* an apartment over the restaurant."

"Oh … yeah, I guess she didn't say that exactly. She just said she moved in upstairs. So I assumed there was an apartment. Anyway, the point is, something's obviously wrong. She very clearly said *she and Caleb.* No mention of Mister."

"His name is Greg. And you're gossiping."

"Am *not!*" she cried in defense, while simultaneously realizing he was right—she *was* gossiping. "I'm just concerned for Caleb."

"Sure," James said, dragging the word out to show his disbelief.

"Do you know anything about it? Has Greg said anything?"

James took a big bite of pizza crust and then looked at her. He chewed, swallowed, and said, "Men don't talk about that stuff."

His tone added, "Men don't care about that stuff."

Chapter 3

Church was *packed*. Every Sunday it seemed there were new people. Emily wondered where they were all coming from. Today, much to Emily's surprise, Jane Crockett was sitting in the back row with her daughter, Sara—Emily's favorite outfielder. Emily didn't get to church in time to talk to them or deliver hugs, but she did send an excited wave, which caused both of them to look embarrassed. Emily was thrilled they were there, wondered who had invited them, and felt guilty for not inviting them herself.

Outgrowing a space is a good problem for a church body to have, Emily realized, but it made for an uncomfortable Sunday morning meeting. She and James had arrived just late enough to miss getting actual chairs and went to lean against a wall. This part she could deal with. The bad part was, though it was nice and cool when they first entered, by the end of the service, the basement became hot and muggy. There was no ventilation, and only one exit, found at the top of a rickety set of stairs. At the end of a service, she couldn't wait to get out of there and breathe some fresh air, but it took at least twenty minutes for everyone to file out through the bottleneck. Each Sunday, she would resist the urge to trample the senior citizens.

More than once, she had mentioned to James, as well as Abe and Lily, that they should meet outside during the summer, but nothing had ever come of it. She wasn't sure why. Maybe lobstermen felt they already spent enough time outside.

On this particular Sunday, someone else broached the issue.

A man Emily knew only as Scott stood up during announcement time and asked, "Could we please talk about the building?"

Abe, who was up front, put one hand up as if to stop him from speaking and said, "I don't think this is a good time, Scott. Maybe we could all chat after the service."

Scott seemed satisfied with this and sat down. But all through the worship music and the message, Emily's curiosity distracted her. What had he meant by "the building"? What building? As in there already was one? Or as in the word was a gerund—someone planned to build, and that was "the building" referenced. She couldn't be the only one wondering. Maybe they *should* have talked it over when Scott brought it up—get it out of the way.

But it turned out few people cared about what Scott had to say. At least not enough to endure the muggy basement air. Most of the congregation filed slowly up the stairs.

Abe gave them a few minutes to exit, and Emily took this opportunity to talk to Sara and her mom. She gave them each a big hug and said, "Welcome! I'm so thrilled to see you here. What did you think?"

Jane gave her an ambiguous "It was fine." Sara just shrugged. But Sara didn't really like anything—except centerfield.

"How is Duke?" Emily asked, referring to Jane's son, who was currently at the youth corrections center because he threatened to blow up the island's windmills. "Have you heard from him?"

Jane's face lit up at the mention of his name. "He calls home every week. He's doing OK, considering ..." Her voice trailed off.

"Well, let him know that I think of him and pray for him often, next time you talk to him."

TRESPASS

"Thank you. I will." Jane turned to go and then turned back. "And that does mean a lot, Miss Morse. Thank you."

"Please, call me Emily," she said and then watched them get in line at the bottom of the stairs.

Abe returned to the front of the room. "OK, Scott, what did you want to talk about?"

James had finally found some empty seats, and Emily sat beside him.

Scott did not stand up, but spoke from his seat, "Well, as you know, Abe, some of us have been talking …"

Emily knew no such thing. Who had been talking? And when? And why didn't James know? He started this church. Or maybe he did know, but he just hadn't said anything to her about it. She stole a look at his face, but it offered no information.

Scott was still talking. "I just think it's not very welcoming to have guests squash in here like sardines. I don't even like to invite people anymore, because I know they probably won't get a seat. It just makes sense to start talking about building. I know it will be expensive, but I think if we all work together, God will make a way."

No one said anything at first, but then Abe said, "I just don't know how to go about starting such a project, Scott. It's not that I don't want to. It's not that I want to keep this church in my cellar forever." Abe chuckled at his own joke.

James spoke up. "You may not care, Abe, but I do. If you're talking about starting from scratch and building a new building, that is a giant waste of resources."

Scott's wife gasped, and Emily herself was surprised at the passion in James's voice.

Scott's face grew red. "What are you talking about? How could a new house for God be a waste of resources?"

James didn't even hesitate. "Because there are people on this island who are hungry. There are people who cannot heat their homes in the winter. People who can't pay for the medications they need. Last winter we were able to help those people. We won't be able to if we're paying off a mortgage."

"No one said anything about a mortgage, Gagnon," Scott said.

Why do men call each other by their last names? Especially when they're angry? Are they trying to be football players? Or soldiers? Football playing soldiers?

"How else are you going to pay for a brand-new building?" James asked dryly. "None of us even own any land." James did own land, the eighth of an acre his house was built on, but she knew what he meant. She also knew Piercehaven land wasn't cheap.

Scott didn't say anything. Evidently, he didn't have a financial plan.

Someone else did speak up. Emily vaguely thought his name was Gunner. "If God wants this to happen, he will give us the funds."

James said, "The fact that we don't have the funds makes me think God doesn't want this to happen. But I'm not just trying to be a naysayer. There is another way, an easier way, I think. And a better way."

Scott made a disgusted grunting sound. "And what way might that be?"

James's jaw tightened, and Emily knew Scott had ruffled his feathers. "In the New Testament," James said, and it sounded as though he was struggling to keep his voice even, "people met in homes. Jesus never told anyone to go build a white building with a steeple, and Paul never said that either—"

"You're going to pretend the temple never existed?" Scott interrupted.

"The temple was *Jewish*," James said. "Jesus came to build a new church, which is what we are, unless you just forgot to wear your kippah today?"

Scott furrowed his brow in confusion.

James continued, "I'm not trying to fight. I just think it's a *really* bad idea to undertake a big building project. What sets us apart from other churches is the fact that we *don't* have a building. People are more likely to walk in here than into a building that makes them feels churchy. They associate church with being judged. They associate us with a bunch of people they already know who happen to hang out in a basement. I hope they'll come to just associate us with Jesus. And our tithes and offerings are able to go to actual people, not upkeep on a building, not property tax, not heating a building we're only going to use once a week."

"We'd use it more than once a week," Scott said, as if James were a moron.

"We still wouldn't use it enough to justify heating it in January."

Scott looked at Abe, his eyes pleading with Abe to side with him. Abe looked at James. "So there's another way?"

"Yes." James took a deep breath. "We multiply."

At first, no one said anything, but then Scott said, "You mean we split?"

"No." James was no longer trying to hide his anger. "That is *not* what I mean. Don't put words in my mouth. We started this in my house. Maybe those who live close to me can come back there. Those who live closer to Abe can come here—"

"That's foolish," Scott spat. "Why would you split us up? We're a family!"

Abe held up a hand again. "Let him finish."

"We'd still be a family. But this is how they're doing it all over the world—"

"This is how *who's* doing it?" Scott interrupted again.

"Missionaries. Church planters. When a body outgrows a home, they split into two, and then they continue to grow. Then when those two outgrow their homes, they split again, and there are four groups. This is how churches multiply."

"We're not in Africa," Scott mumbled.

Everyone ignored that particular comment.

"Gotta admit," Abe said, "that does sound a lot simpler. It's not like we're never going to see these people again."

Emily felt a little sick. Did her church just get moved into the house that would soon be hers? Was she going to be hosting *church services* as a newlywed? She wasn't sure how she felt about that.

"I'll tell you what," Abe said. "Let's not decide anything right now. Let's cool off, seek God about this, and we'll talk again next week."

"Or we could have a meeting on Tuesday," Scott said. "Whatever we decide, we should do it soon, or we're going to have people on your lawn trying to hear what's going on inside."

"I have a game Tuesday night," James muttered.

"No problem," Abe said. "When would you like to meet, James?"

"Wednesday after four?"

"Great. Let's meet at six. We can meet here. Spread the word. Anyone who wants to talk about it, let's talk about it. Until then"—he looked at the two men before him with sober eyes—"take it to God."

Chapter 4

Emily returned to the pizzeria on Monday evening. She brought her "wedding planner notebook" with her, even though it had precious little in it. James *had* finally given her his list, so she had that: a total of twenty-two names. Far fewer than he would have garnered had he gone with the word of mouth approach.

When she first entered the restaurant, it appeared deserted, but Kim soon materialized behind the counter. "Hiya, Emily. Would you like some food, or should we just get right to work?"

Even though the overpowering scent of pepperoni made Emily's mouth water, she managed to shake her head. "Maybe later."

"Great." Kim grabbed a pen and pad of paper, came around the counter, and slid into a booth, all while wearing an excited smile.

Emily thought maybe she'd missed her calling. "Can I keep you on retainer for every kid's birthday party too?"

Kim's eyes lit up. "Absolutely. I've already done a few high school graduation parties. I told you I love this stuff."

Emily slid into the booth across from her. "Did you tell Caleb you were doing this?"

Kim nodded. "I spoke the words, but I'm not sure he heard me." She curled her lip. "Video games."

"Ah. So is he fishing much this summer?"

"Every day. He's got his own boat and everything. He's doing great. He's tried to offer to support me, but I won't let him. I'm trying to convince him to save his money, in case he ever wants to do something other than fish."

"Does he show any interest in anything else?" Emily certainly hadn't seen him do so.

Kim's face fell. "Not yet, no. So, how about your wedding?"

"Sure." Emily opened her notebook. "But I just wanted to say that I'm sorry your life is complicated right now. If there's anything I can do—"

"Thanks," Kim said quickly, "but we're fine."

"Even so, sometimes people just need other people. And our basement church is full of helpful, loving people. If you ever need anything, they will help, and you're welcome there anytime."

Kim gave her a quick, small smile. "So, what are you planning on for flowers?"

"I was thinking wildflowers. I was going to go out the day before and pick—"

"No way. Too much of a gamble. Plus, you're not going to have time"—she scribbled on her notepad. Emily tried to see what she was writing, but couldn't make it out—"I'll send someone over to the mainland the day before and get some real flowers. What's your budget?"

Emily was flummoxed. "Uh … who? I mean, who are you going to send on a three-hour voyage for *my* flowers?"

Kim shrugged. "I have people. Don't worry about it."

"But I do," Emily said quickly. "I mean, we're not inviting a lot of islanders. I don't want to accidentally be beholden to someone and then not invite them."

Kim put a hand on Emily's. "Didn't you just tell me that it's important to let people help? There are people who will help, without expecting anything. Don't forget, lots of people on this island really appreciate what you did for our girls last winter."

Emily's mouth fell open. "What? I thought people hated me for that."

"The *loud* people hated you for that. The obnoxious ones. And some of them changed their tune once Milton confessed to everything. Plus, you know, *state championship*. Anyway, forget those people. I'm talking about the kind people who were never out to get you. Especially the ones with young daughters. Trust me. You'll have flowers. Now, what's your budget?"

Emily didn't know. "A hundred dollars?"

Kim barked out a laugh, sounding like a snarky Chihuahua. "Seriously?"

Emily knew her cheeks were getting pink. "I don't know. How much do we need?"

"How many bridesmaids do you have?"

Emily closed her eyes. She was so out of her element. She longed to be grading papers instead, something she was good at. She'd been a bridesmaid twice, but each of those had been relatively traumatic experiences with giant wedding parties. "I don't know," she finally said. "I was just planning to have as many bridesmaids as James was going to have groomsmen."

Kim paused, as if waiting for Emily to elaborate. When she didn't, "And how many groomsmen does he want to have?"

"Uh …" Of course she didn't know.

Kim shook her head, dramatizing her disapproval. "Forget him for a second. I know you're marrying the guy, and he's wonderful and all that, but for planning purposes, I want you to forget all about him. Capiche?"

Emily giggled. The idea made her feel a little, well, *renegade*. "OK."

"Good. Now, how many bridesmaids do you want?"

Emily still had no idea. Her only sister had made it clear she wanted nothing to do with it. She had a thousand cousins. She couldn't invite one of them, or she'd have to invite them all. "One?"

Kim's brow furrowed. "Seriously?"

"Naomi. My best friend growing up. She should be there. But I think if I go beyond that, the dam will break, and I'll have a thousand."

"OK, then. One bridesmaid." She scribbled again. "Then sure, maybe we can do flowers for a hundred. I'll make some calls. Now. About Pig Poop Point." She put her pen down and leveled a gaze at Emily. She looked so serious, Emily had to laugh. "How committed are you to that location?"

Emily was pretty committed. "I don't know?"

"How about the beach?"

"The *public* beach?" Emily assumed that would be extremely busy in August.

"Yes. Although I think the *public* would clear out of the way if we set up an arbor and a bunch of chairs."

Emily chewed on that for several seconds. "I did think it would be cool to be barefoot."

"I don't want you to be barefoot. James is too tall. But if you insist, you definitely shouldn't be barefoot on Pig Poop. Unless you want to slice your toe open on a barnacle. There's much more parking at the beach. Still not enough, probably, but we can shuttle people if we need to ..." She looked down at her notebook and then back at Emily. "How many guests?"

Emily knew this one. She flipped open her own notebook. "Seventy."

"Only seventy?" Kim looked concerned.

"Why do you look like that?"

She looked at the ceiling, as if carefully considering her next words. "And how many of those people are islanders?"

Emily looked down at her notebook, and then back up to Kim's anxious eyes. "Twenty-two?" She said it like a question, as if she was asking permission for that number to be acceptable. Then she kept talking, "James's list has his parents, his best friend, well I assume he's his best friend, he just calls him his 'buddy,' but I mean Brent Clawford, you must know him ... So, Brent's family, plus James's brother and his family ..." She was getting confused, so she looked down at her list. "And the Cafferty family, and then James's aunt, uncle, and cousins, and I think that's it." She scanned the list. James hadn't written it in any particular order, so she wanted to make sure she hadn't missed anyone.

"Uh-huh," Kim said and appeared to be doing some deep analytical thinking. "And how many islanders are on your half of the list?"

She knew the answer to this, but she looked down at her list anyway, feeling a little ashamed of the answer. Finally, she looked back up into Kim's expectant eyes. "None."

"Uh-huh," Kim said again. She leaned back in the booth.

"Well, you're invited. Now."

Kim laughed. "You don't have to invite me. Really. Though Caleb will want to go if Chloe's going."

"Really? Why?" Emily was shocked. She knew of no connection between those two kids and didn't like the idea of something going on without her knowledge.

"He's quite sweet on her."

"Oh." Emily was relieved. So the situation didn't really involve Chloe directly. Therefore, she didn't need to feel bad about not being consulted about it.

"And it seems the feeling goes both ways."

"Oh." Now she was sad. She decided then that she didn't like summer vacation. She was missing too much of her students' lives. She suddenly missed Thomas and Chloe terribly and wondered how Thomas felt about Chloe and Caleb. She wondered if Chloe was doing something to make Thomas jealous, and vowed to ask Chloe at church. She realized Kim was talking. "I'm sorry, what?"

"I said that, while I understand why you would want to focus on inviting your family, if you don't invite anyone from the island, you might offend someone."

Emily nodded. "I thought about that, but it's just like with the bridesmaids, isn't it? Once I invite one of them, I'll have to invite them all?"

Kim scrunched up her face. "That's a good point. And I suppose we could just say that you're the one inviting the Caffertys. But what about people you work with? Haven't you made any teacher friends?"

"Not really. They're not a very friendly bunch. I really like the art teacher, but again, invite her—"

TRESPASS

"And you've got to invite them all. OK. I see your point. So for now, let's go with seventy. And most of them won't need parking, because they're coming on the ferry. You might want to tell them not to bring their cars. If they do, we're going to have a wicked hard time getting them all back *off* the island all at the same time. As I'm sure you know, the ferries are *packed* on August weekends."

Emily knew no such thing, but now that she'd heard it, she wasn't surprised.

"So," Kim said, "let's talk about what really matters—food. How do you feel about Italian?"

Chapter 5

Tuesday evening found Emily back in the school gym. She didn't exactly love this part of her summer, but she wanted to be with James, and she did enjoy getting to check in with her girls. So she sat on the end of the bench, saying encouraging things to the girls and doing her best to keep track of statistics she didn't really understand. Why did James need to know how many rebounds Hannah had in a summer basketball game against Valley? She had no idea. But she was counting them, nonetheless.

Hailey and Hannah were going into their senior year. Emily could hardly believe it. And, though this was only summer basketball, they both seemed to be taking basketball more seriously now. Emily hadn't thought Hailey could get more serious about basketball, but she was looking at it right now, and was a bit alarmed.

Emily would lose a lot of her favorites in the spring of this coming year. Thomas and Noah were going to be seniors too. She could hear Kyle the social studies teacher's voice in her head: *Don't worry. They don't actually go anywhere. They just come to school less often.* But she thought he was wrong about Hailey and Thomas. She thought they would be going places. She didn't know much about basketball, admittedly, but she thought Hailey was good enough to play at just about any college in the country. And Thomas? Well, Thomas was just too smart and too charming to spend the rest of his life on Piercehaven. *Nothing against Piercehaven, of course.*

Speaking of her favorites, MacKenzie and Chloe—cousins by blood and sisters by Christ—were both going to be juniors. As Emily watched MacKenzie, who was also her catcher in the spring, bring the ball up the court as point guard, she was again amazed at the unassuming maturity in that young woman.

Sydney Hopkins, daughter of obnoxious school board member Kermit (PeeWee) Hopkins, was no longer a freshman and was bossing everyone around the court. Emily wondered when James was going to put a stop to that.

Victoria, also going into her sophomore year, was warming the bench at the moment, but Emily knew that wasn't a long-term arrangement.

Caleb Aronson, also soon to be a sophomore, sat alone on the opposite side of the gym, watching Chloe's every move. He was careful to avoid eye contact with Emily, probably because he found it awkward that his mom's new best friend was his English teacher. Emily and Caleb had never been particularly tight. She hoped that might change now.

Zoe Lane was the sole freshman on the team, and two eighth graders and two seventh graders rounded out the lineup. It was a good thing it doesn't take many athletes to make a basketball team, because Piercehaven didn't have many to spare. It was more difficult to field a softball team, which needed at least nine players, but playing Piercehaven softball was far less of a commitment than playing Piercehaven basketball. Emily didn't even think they should use the word "playing" when it came to their winter sport—it was more like obsessing.

TRESPASS

The buzzer sounded for halftime, and James gave the girls a quick, calm pep talk at the bench before sending them back out to shoot around for a few minutes.

"I meant to ask you," he said, sitting down beside her, and his tone told her that he needed something.

"Yes?"

"Can you host a few girls on Thursday night?" The last ferry left the island before basketball games ended, so visiting athletes were hosted by islanders for the night, and then caught the ferry in the morning.

She stopped herself from groaning. "Sure. Not tonight though?"

"No, I've got tonight covered. Valley girls are staying with MacKenzie, Chloe, and Hailey. But Richmond is on Thursday, and they've got a lot more girls."

Emily sighed. "Okeedoke. I still can't believe they pay to ride the ferry just for a summer basketball game."

"We pay for it," he said, with no inflection in his voice, staring out at his girls.

"Say what?"

He looked at her. "Yeah. Otherwise, we'd get no games. And it's cheaper to bring them out here than for us to go there and stay in motels on the mainland."

"I thought you guys slept on gym floors when you went to away games?"

"Schools are hesitant to let us do that in the summer. I don't know why."

"Oh." She'd never really thought about it, but she guessed, if summer basketball was a necessity, and apparently it was, then this system made some sense.

The buzzer sounded again, and James stood up quickly. For the next sixteen minutes, he would forget that Emily existed. She had accepted this, even sort of understood it.

The Lady Panthers continued to crush the Lady Cavaliers. Valley tried to double team Hailey, but it didn't make any difference. She would either spin out of the trap or just kick the ball out to Chloe, who was shooting .500 from behind the three-point arc. Sydney was ridiculously good on defense and kept stripping the ball from the Valley point guard, who looked as if she just really wanted to go home. Hannah had slidden, seemingly effortlessly, into the center position, and on the rare occasion that Hailey missed, Hannah was there to scoop it up and put it back in—as though she had been born for such an occasion.

Despite enjoying watching the synergy that was the Piercehaven girls' basketball team,

TRESPASS

Emily was glad when the game was over. She closed the scorebook and handed it to her fiancé.

She saw Chloe making gaga eyes at Caleb across the gym. "Hey, Chloe," she said, stepping closer to her. "What's up with you and Caleb?"

Chloe shrugged coyly. "I dunno."

"Are you an item?"

Chloe snickered. "No one says that, Miss Morse. I've tried to tell you that. But yeah, I guess we're going out."

"You guess? What about Thomas?"

"Shh!" Chloe looked panic-stricken, though Emily had spoken quietly enough that no one could possibly have overheard her. "What about him?"

"I thought you had feelings for Thomas."

Chloe rolled her eyes. "An item? Feelings for someone? You sound old, Miss Morse. No, I don't have feelings for Thomas. We're just friends."

Emily was confident this was not true. "OK, I just … I know it's none of my business, but sometimes girls try to make guys jealous, and that never works out the way they hope it will."

Chloe looked at Caleb, who was now crossing the gym toward them. "I'm not doing that, Miss Morse," she said, with a tone that also added, "Go away now."

"All right. Sure do love you, kiddo. Keep me in the loop of your life." She set Chloe free and turned toward James. "I'm starving. Want to go get something to eat?"

"Big Dipper?" He grinned, and she thought her heart might thump right out of her chest.

"Perfect."

Chapter 6

Emily was dreading the Wednesday night church meeting. From the tightness in James's jaw, she guessed he was too. He drove her there in silence, only speaking when he drove past Abe's driveway and parked along the road. "Lot of cars."

Parking at Abe's house was never easy, and she was surprised no one ever complained. The streets on Piercehaven, especially in the more densely populated part of the island near the town docks, were incredibly narrow. One had to put two wheels on a lawn just to get off the road, and if people parked on both sides of the road, the road was effectively blocked to anything but a bicycle. Certainly no snowplow would be getting through. But no one was thinking about snowplows in June, and James managed to get his truck far enough onto Abe's neighbor's lawn that someone could probably get by if they needed to.

James took her hand and side by side they headed toward Abe's door. As soon as they opened it, they could hear a bunch of animated voices coming from below. *Oh great. They're already wound up.*

Descending the stairs, she could see why there'd been so many cars: there were a lot of people. Scott and his family were there. As were Gunner and his. Noah and McKenzie sat hand-in-hand beside her mom. Chloe and her parents were there. Did this many people really care about whether they were going to build a church? Emily gave James a wide-eyed look, and then led them to a couple of vacant chairs. She looked around for Abe and found him sitting in the front row, looking worried. Chloe's mom, Gina, was having an intense conversation with Scott's wife, and Emily strained to overhear, but she couldn't get much because there were so many other people talking at the same time. She thought she heard Gina say, "I'm sure he'll go home soon." What? Who would go home?

"If I could have your attention," Abe said from the front of the room. He leaned on a makeshift podium, looking tired. Like many of the men in the room, he'd just gotten back from hauling traps. "We scheduled this meeting to talk about whether or not we want to pursue building. I'd rather focus on that, and not the Nautikus fella, but if we have to talk about him, let's do it quickly and try to honor God."

The room fell silent. Emily didn't know who the Nautikus fella was, but evidently it was difficult to talk about him and honor God at the same time.

"Who's the Nautikus fella?" Emily muttered to James, even though she didn't think he knew either.

"Tell you later."

James knew things. James always knew things.

"All right then," Abe said. "Scott is going to say a few things, and then James will."

Scott, even though he hadn't been invited to do so, went to the front of the room and took Abe's spot, unfolding a piece of notebook paper as he went. He cleared his throat. "First things first, I don't want to fight. I just want what's best for my family." He looked down at his paper, which was visibly trembling in his hand. "I have a vision for our future. I see a small, simple church somewhere with a big yard. We could have a playground, and rooms for Sunday school, and maybe even a youth group. Maybe even a small gym. We could have big meals together there, and have

46

ministries for children and seniors. We could fundraise, and I found an organization that lends to churches for a rate of three percent. We could even get a church name, so we would no longer have to be called the church that meets in Abe's basement." He looked up at the small crowd and laughed. Apparently, that last bit was a joke, but no one laughed. He stood there for an uncomfortable few seconds, then said, "Thank you," and sat down.

James stood and headed toward the front. He had no piece of paper. He did have his Bible. He turned and faced his audience and took a deep breath. "Can we just pray?" Without waiting for an answer, he bowed his head. "Father, I know you are here with us right now, and I just ask you to fill us all with wisdom. Give each of us the mind of Christ so that we can think in unity. We want your will to be done, not mine, and not anyone else's, only yours. So please make your will crystal clear to us. Thank you. In Jesus' name, amen."

He opened his eyes and then he opened his Bible. "I've spent a lot of time seeking God about this, and I just want to share a few Scriptures with you. It's occurred to me that God is in the business of multiplying. He's been doing it since Genesis. It's what he does.

TRESPASS

In Genesis 1:28, God told Adam and Eve in the garden to be fruitful and multiply, fill the whole earth. I don't think he was just talking about making babies." A few people giggled at this, even though Emily was certain James hadn't meant it to be funny. "I think he was talking about making more of *his people*, more people *for him.* This was before the fall, right? So I think he was saying, 'Make more children *for me.*' Then, later in Genesis, God gives Abraham the best promise Abraham could've imagined. He said he would multiply his seed like the stars of the heaven. Again, not just people, but *God's people.* We are part of a result of that promise. We are part of that multiplication, and we are still multiplying. Otherwise we would still fit in this basement like we did our first Sunday here, with room to spare. But thank God we have this problem. In Acts 12:24"—he flipped to the New Testament—"it's talking about the early church and it says 'The word of the Lord continued to grow and to be multiplied.' I'm not trying to twist Scripture here, but I can't help but notice that it doesn't say, 'The word of the Lord grew in one place and had programs.'" He took a deep breath.

Emily wasn't sure where he was going with all this, and wasn't sure she'd agree with him when he got there, but she sure was proud of him. He was speaking with a gentle authority. He was going to make such a good dad.

"I subscribe to a lot of missionary publications, and *none* of the missionaries build big fancy churches at the edge of town—"

Scott tried to interrupt, but Abe shushed him.

James continued, "Missionaries plant churches. And I'm not just talking about in Africa. Missionaries in America do the same thing. Statistics show that the majority of people who come to a new church plant are those who *weren't going to church at all*. They don't come from other churches. They come from their couches on Sunday mornings. This tells me that there are people out there who are nervous about walking into an already established group of believers, but plant a new church, and new people will feel more comfortable walking in, if nothing else but to see what it's all about. I think that's what made this group grow so fast—it felt easy to walk into Abe's basement. Not so easy to walk into a building with a steeple, because people have all these preconceptions about churches." He took another big breath. "I'll stop now, but I have a vision too, Scott"—he looked him in the eye—"and that is to have a house church on every single block in this town, on every road on this island, so that whenever anyone has a need, has a crisis, they have somewhere close to go, someone they know to go to, and in that way, we can minister to everyone on this island, not just to each other. Thank you."

He returned to his seat, and Emily thought her chest might burst with pride. He'd almost convinced her of his reasoning, and she'd really wanted a church nursery.

Scott stood up again, uninvited this time, and spoke from his current spot. "What about events that would draw those people in? Free suppers? Youth group pizza parties? Concerts—"

Gunner interrupted. "We can do all those things from our homes, if we're willing, Scott." He looked at James. "You're right, Gagnon. I never would've stepped foot in a church building. But when Abe invited me to his house, I was curious enough to come. And now I've given my life to God, never been happier, and can't wait to come to church on Sunday. I'm with you."

James nodded and gave him a tight smile.

Abe stood back up. "Does anyone else want to say anything?"

"I think we should vote," Scott said.

Gunner flashed a glare at him. "Are you angling to get some work out of this? Is that what this is all about?"

"Don't be stupid," Scott said, but his face flushed red.

Emily leaned to James's ear. "Is he a carpenter?" she asked through closed teeth.

James nodded.

"I don't think we should vote yet," Abe said. "Let's all take it to prayer. I'd like to pray about it again right now, and if anyone else wants to, go ahead, don't be shy. Then I say we take some time, maybe a week or so, and then we'll talk about it again. If we all listen to the Holy Spirit, we should all be able to agree, and not even need a vote. He's not going to tell each of us different things."

Emily was annoyed. She didn't think they needed to talk it to death. Why not just make a decision? But she stayed quiet on the matter.

Abe prayed, gave a chance for others to pray, and when no one did, said, "Amen."

Gunner opened his eyes and said, "Now can we talk about the Nautikus punk?"

"His name is Kevin," Abe said, "and I'm not sure talking about the situation would be useful."

"How do you know his name?" Gunner asked.

TRESPASS

Abe glanced at his son. "Kids know everything. He's Kevin Linville, and he's dating Harley Hopkins."

"Obviously," Gunner said with a sneer. "She was on the boat."

"And did you see this for yourself?" Abe asked with a raised eyebrow that said he doubted it.

Gunner didn't answer.

"I know the situation is irritating right now, but PeeWee knows how things work 'round here." Abe pronounced "here" as "he-ah." "He'll get it taken care of."

"I heard PeeWee gave him permission!" Gunner said loudly, and several people groaned.

Abe pounded his podium with one fist, as if he wished he had a gavel. "This is what I *don't* want to do here. We shouldn't be gossiping, and we shouldn't be stirring up ill will toward this young man. It will work itself out. No one needs to panic."

"I'm going to panic with my knife on his lines," Gunner said, and several people laughed.

I'd give my right arm to know what they're talking about, Emily thought. She couldn't wait to get James alone and get the scoop, gossiping or not.

Chapter 7

Relaxing in her hammock with her nose in the new Ted Dekker book, Emily lost track of time and barely made it to the gym for Thursday's tipoff. James greeted her with a scowl that made her wish she'd never climbed out of the hammock.

But after a few grumpy minutes, she settled into her spot on the bleachers and her job with the stats. Rebounds, steals, and assists— earth-shattering stuff.

There were more spectators tonight, even some she didn't know. *Must be Richmond parents*, she thought, and then, *Those are some dedicated parents.*

After the game, she quickly asked James, "I'm not hosting parents, am I?"

He gave her the same scowl, ticking her off even more this time. "No, why?"

"Because that's even more uncomfortable than hosting children."

"No, they're staying at the Airbnb."

"We *have* an Airbnb?" She couldn't believe it.

James's face lit up.

"What? Why are you smiling at me?" She was suspicious.

"Because you said, 'we.' Not 'you' or 'the island,' but 'we.'" He bent to kiss her on the cheek.

The strangest things made this man happy, but she'd take it.

"The Airbnb just opened. I thought we could go there for our honeymoon." He laughed.

She didn't.

"You just have two girls"—he looked at his clipboard—"Alyssa and Sage."

"Okeedoke. So ..." She tried to think of something to say. "How was work?"

He glowered. "*He* was out there again today."

She didn't need to ask who the offending "he" was. James had filled her in on the way home from the church meeting. PeeWee Hopkin's oldest daughter, Harley, had a new beau. From the island of Nautikus. Apparently, dating someone from Nautikus was a significant crime. An even more significant crime was bringing his boat from his island to theirs and fishing in their waters. There was a slightly gray area because Harley *did* have the right to fish there, but not in "a boat from away"—James's words. James thought she was just hanging out anyway, so that her boyfriend could technically fish there. She'd never shown any interest in fishing in her life, according to James.

"I'm sorry," Emily said, because she didn't know what else to say.

James shrugged. "Not much we can do about it, I guess. But it's *so* disrespectful. I wouldn't be surprised if PeeWee gets his teeth knocked out sometime soon."

"Right, in one of Piercehaven's dark alleys?" She grinned. Piercehaven didn't have any alleys.

He didn't think she was funny.

"Why does Harley even have a fishing license? Aren't they hard to get?"

"They are now. But back in the day, lobstermen always bought them for their kids when they turned five. That's how I got mine."

Emily's jaw dropped. "*Five?*"

James nodded. "They don't let you do it anymore, but Harley's had a license her whole life. But that girl hasn't fished. She never fished with her dad. She never fished by herself. I don't even think she could drop a trap if she had to. So it doesn't count that she's just floating around with this guy now. She can go fish with him off his island."

"Why doesn't she?"

James shrugged. "No one in their right mind would go live out there."

Emily snickered. She'd heard the same about her current home.

James seemed to sense her confusion. "Nautikus is *out* there. Twenty-five miles off the mainland."

"That's farther out than Matinicus, isn't it?"

"Yep. Totally isolated. And the people are weird."

Hello, Pot. My name is Kettle.

"I wouldn't want to live there," he said.

Well, no, James, you wouldn't want to live anywhere *but here.* "I see."

He gave her a skeptical look.

"What?" she asked, feeling defensive.

"No, you don't see. It's obvious. But trust me. This is a big deal, and PeeWee and this Linville guy are not being very smart. Someone's going to get hurt."

Emily thought for a second. "It's a sin to think this, but I wouldn't be too upset if someone knocked PeeWee's teeth out. Still, I wouldn't want anyone to get in trouble over this. You can't just go around punching people."

"Actually, if someone's fishing in your waters, you can."

The girls came out of the locker room then, in a pack, and Emily didn't get a chance to respond to James's ominous pronouncement. James matched the Bobcats up with their island hosts, and Emily, all hospitable smiles that she didn't really feel, showed them to her car.

As she pressed the fob button that chirped and unlocked her car, one of the girls said, "Aren't you the softball coach?"

Ugh. Even more awkward.

"I am. Do you play?"

"I'm the catcher," Alyssa said, sounding offended that Emily didn't recognize her.

Sorry, when I saw you last, your face was wearing a cage. "Oh, OK. Nice to see you again."

"Yeah." Alyssa slid into the front seat, not even offering it to her teammate, who wordlessly got into the back. "You guys were good this year."

"Thank you."

"I play softball too," Sage said sheepishly from the back.

"Oh yeah?" Emily looked in her rearview mirror. "What position?"

"Left dugout bench."

All three of them laughed at that, and a lot of the tension slipped away. Emily wondered if she would ever get used to this. Hosting in the summer was way more awkward than hosting in the winter, because the girls got to her house so much earlier, and the sun went down so much later. She couldn't say, "Good night" before the sun went down, could she? What was she supposed to do with them?

"Did you guys have any plans for the evening?"

"I'm happy to just watch TV," Alyssa said.

Emily didn't have a television, so she didn't say anything.

She pulled into her driveway, and the girls spilled out. She headed straight for her phone and dialed The Pizza Place, where, she was thankful, Kim answered. "Ah, got to feed some hungry basketball players?"

Emily could hear the smile in her voice. "It's more than that, and feel free to say no way. Do you have television?"

"Of course. Who doesn't have TV? I've got two hundred channels and Netflix."

Emily let out a long breath. "Would you mind if we ate our pizza in your apartment? I've got no way to entertain these kids." She could see the girls standing in her living room, pretending they weren't trying to overhear their conversation.

"Of course. Caleb would *love* that. Come on over. I'll get the pizzas in the oven."

"Thank you, thank you, thank you."

"You bet. Not a big deal. Really. I've hosted before. I get it."

She tried to stretch the phone cord into the living room. She almost made it. "What kind of pizza would you like?"

"I'm gluten-free," Alyssa said.

Emily fought the urge to roll her eyes. Gluten-free children should bring their own food. "Kim, can you do—"

"I heard her. Yes. We've got gluten-free. Ask her if she's got Celiac, though. I'm supposed to ask, as Dad wants to avoid a lawsuit."

"Do you have Celiac?"

"No, I just don't like gluten," she said, and collapsed on Emily's couch, sending Emily's cat, Nick Carraway, who was resting on the back of the couch, up the spiral staircase as if his tail was on fire.

"Your gluten-free will be fine," Emily said, striving for tonelessness, into the phone.

"All right. I'll see you in a few. Good luck."

Chapter 8

On Sunday morning, Emily was thrilled to see Kim and Caleb coming down Abe's basement stairs. She'd invited them multiple times now, but she didn't think they'd actually come. Then she saw Caleb make a beeline for Chloe, and was less surprised. Kim stood at the bottom of the stairs, abandoned by her son, looking overwhelmed. Emily waved her over.

Kim got there just in time, before the Parkers took over the rest of the row. They were a huge family. Emily had tried to count their kids before, but they wouldn't hold still, so she'd never gotten a proper roster.

Kim sat, and Emily patted her on the knee, trying to reel in her own excitement—didn't want to scare another one off. "How are you?"

"Not that good," she said frankly. "That's why I'm here. Chloe invited Caleb, and I thought, why not? My life can't get much worse."

Emily had no words.

Kim looked at her, flashed her a quick, obviously-forced smile, and then looked front again. "Don't worry. I'm being dramatic. Things are just hard right now."

"I'm so sorry."

Kim sighed. "It'll be OK. Probably. I just miss my home. Caleb's always grumpy. He's torn between his parents. And I can't believe I'm living with my parents again. I'm almost forty for crying out loud. I'm grateful for their help, but they're driving me nuts."

Emily strained, but, much to her frustration, couldn't think of anything encouraging or comforting to say. "Is there any hope for reconciliation?"

Kim looked at her quickly. "I don't think so. The man is married to his boat and to his bottle, in that order. I don't even make the list."

Please, Father, give me words.

"Though Caleb says he has quit drinking. Or at least, that's what he's telling his son. I have no idea if that's true."

"Does Caleb see him often?"

"Every day. They have separate boats, but they see each other at the docks."

"Do they fish near each other?" Emily had a romantic vision of father and son lobster boats idling side-by-side.

"Not really. Caleb fishes where his grandfather fished."

The worship team, which was only a keyboard player and a guitarist, started the music, and everyone stood up. Kim was slow to rise and looked as if she already regretted her decision to come to church.

Emily was thrilled to hear that the music was excellent that morning. That wasn't always the case. Neither musicians were close to professionals, and both were just doing the best they could, but Emily was hoping that, since they were both playing in the same key today, Kim would be able to focus on the music's message.

The music faded, and everyone sat down. Abe got up to welcome everyone, and to open with prayer. When Emily opened her eyes, she saw that Scott was standing beside Abe up front, and she suppressed a groan. Now what?

Abe also looked surprised, as if Scott had snuck up on him while he'd been praying. Emily thought that if this was the case, that would be pretty hilarious.

"I have something to share," Scott said authoritatively.

Abe stared at him, expressionless, as if deciding what to say.

Scott didn't wait for his permission. He looked at the room. "James shared some statistics at our last meeting, and I've done some research, and I just wanted to share a few of my own." He read from a trembling piece of paper in his hand, and spoke quickly, lest anyone have a chance to object. "Churches with active children's ministries have 150 percent more attendance. Churches with youth groups have 100 percent more attendance than those without ..." Emily looked at James, who, to his credit, she thought, appeared to be respectfully giving Scott his attention. "... and churches that have weekly suppers see 20 percent more attendance on Sundays." He looked up. "Just wanted you to think about that as you all are trying to decide which direction you want this church to take." Scott sat down.

"Where'd you get those statistics?" Gunner asked, with more volume than necessary.

Scott sat and looked at Gunner. "What?"

"Where did you get those numbers? Did you just make them up?"

"I got them online."

Gunner laughed at this. So did a few others. "Well, obviously," Gunner said, "but what website? A company selling children's programs?"

"Hey, hey, hey." Abe held both hands up. "We'll have another special meeting for this discussion. Right now, Darius has prepared a message for us."

During the short sermon, Emily kept trying to steal discreet glimpses of Kim's face, but she looked consistently bored throughout. And when it was over, she looked relieved.

Abe stood up to thank everyone and to close in prayer. The second he finished, a dozen people swarmed around Scott. Even though they were trying to keep their voices low, Emily could hear the heat coming off their words.

"What's up with all that?" Kim asked, her curious eyes on the huddle.

"So here's the thing about Christians," Emily said. "Sometimes we're idiots."

Kim's face lit up for the first time that morning. "What?"

"Yeah, it's true. We have received God's gift, which is saving our souls, and that gift does transform us into new creations, but the transformation isn't always quick. We all still have to struggle with our old selves, and sometimes our motivations get skewed."

Kim looked at the men. Then she looked at Emily. "Skewed might be a good word for it." She looked around the room. "You know I've known most of these people my whole life, right?"

Emily nodded.

"So it's hard for me to accept that Gunner is now some godly man just because he hangs out in Abe's basement on Sundays."

Emily laughed. "He's not godly because he hangs out in a basement. He's godly because of what Jesus did on the cross."

Kim held up a hand. "OK, I think I've heard enough about the cross for one day. No offense, but no thanks." She turned and scanned the room. Emily figured she was looking for Caleb.

"He's probably already gone outside with Chloe."

"OK then, I'm going to go find him. Thanks for letting me sit with you."

"Of course. And Kim, are you going to be OK? I hate to see you upset."

Kim gave her the same quick, fake smile. "I'll be fine. I've got your wedding to distract me. Let's talk tomorrow. I've got some ideas about the menu."

"OK." Emily watched her go, remembering suddenly that she hadn't yet told James they were having the reception catered by the island's pizza joint.

Chapter 9

Tuesday was Emily's first Fourth of July on the island. She wasn't sure what to expect. The day certainly didn't begin much differently for James. He began his country's birthday the way he began every day: at the dock before dawn.

But he had promised her a barbeque that afternoon, and she was looking forward to it. So much so that she was having trouble keeping herself entertained that day. She puttered around doing housework and then tried to assume her backyard-hammock-reading position, but she had trouble focusing on the words. She just wanted to be in his arms, watching fireworks in the sky. *Gosh, I can't wait to marry that man.*

Finally, four o'clock rolled around, and, after changing outfits three times, she headed for her car and for "downtown" Piercehaven. She stopped at the only grocery store to buy some coleslaw, and then headed for James's house, which would soon be her house too.

He was already home. He didn't answer the door, so after standing outside for several long minutes, she just walked in. "I'm here!" she called out, but there was no response. Figuring he was in the shower, she settled onto the couch. On the coffee table in front of her, James's Bible was open to the middle of Acts.

At least he's not reading Revelation again. She scooted forward and began to read.

The angel was just about to bust Peter out of the clink when she realized James was standing over her. Surprised, she looked up. "Hi."

He gave her a giant smile, and bent and kissed her on the top of the head. "Hi yourself."

"You seem happy. I guess your Nautikus intruder wasn't out today?"

"Oh no, he was." He sat down beside her. "I'm just happy to see you." He put his arm around her and pulled her into him. "And I'm trying not to let that guy get to me. He'll get what he's got coming."

She looked up at him. "What does that mean?"

"I don't know yet. But you reap what you sow."

"Does he even know that what he's doing is so wrong?"

James laughed hollowly. "Oh, he knows."

She didn't understand, but she didn't want to think about the errant fisherman either. So she just rested her head on her beloved's chest and enjoyed the rise and fall of it. He smoothed out her hair, making her neck break out in goosebumps.

"So, I've been thinking …" he started.

"Oh yeah?"

"Yeah. I haven't heard you say much about wedding planning lately. Everything OK?"

She sat up and looked at him. This was the first time he'd brought up planning. Ever. "Yes, everything's OK. I just got the impression you didn't really care."

He made a clicking sound with his tongue. "I think I owe you an apology. I didn't really want to deal with the planning stuff. I found it all kind of stressful and just thought we could put it off for a while. But that doesn't mean I don't care about you. Because I do care about you. I love you, and I can't wait to be married to you. But the actual wedding? That's not quite as exciting."

She tried to process this. "OK."

"OK?" he said, and laughed.

"Yeah. OK. I'm not sure what else to say."

"Well … can you forgive me? Are we OK?"

"Of course we're OK."

"And can you forgive me?" he repeated, his eyes twinkling with flirtation.

"I suppose so."

He laughed and pulled her back to his chest. "So where are we at with the planning?"

"We're pretty much done. Kim's been helping me—"

"Kim Aronson?" He sounded shocked. "I wondered why you two were so chummy in church."

"Yes. She offered, and she's really good at it. I think we should have her plan every event we ever have."

He laughed again. "Let's see how this one goes first. So, what's the plan?"

Her stomach did a flip. They had made *so* many decisions without him. She wasn't sure if he was going to be upset. She took a deep breath. "First, we abandoned Pig Poop Point. We're going for the beach instead."

"What?" He sounded surprised, but not upset.

This was good. "Yes. There's not enough parking at Pig Poop, and there are so many rocks. Kim talked me out of it."

"OK. Go on."

"Many of my relatives and friends want to come a day or two early. They say they want to help, but I think they just want to hang out on the island."

"Right," James said slowly, "everyone wants to vacation on the quaint Maine island, till they get here, get bored stiff, and can't wait to get home."

She giggled. "I wish I had a statistic on how many vacationers leave early."

"We could ask the ferry how many reservations get bumped up."

"Speaking of statistics, what did you think of Scott's little speech on Sunday?"

She couldn't see his face, but she could almost feel his eyes roll. "I think that Scott can't even hear himself when he talks. He's not from around here, and it shows."

"How long has he lived here?"

"I don't know, ten years maybe? But I want to talk about the wedding. What else?"

He wants to talk about the wedding. What is going on? "Um … someone named Sally is making the cake—"

"Sally Trimble?"

"I don't know. Someone Kim knows."

"I only know of one Sally on the island, and I can't imagine she knows how to make a wedding cake."

"Shh, don't doubt the wedding planner. Sally will be fine. We're getting a tier of vanilla, a tier of strawberry, and then my tier will be chocolate."

He laughed so quickly, he almost snorted. "You're getting your own *tier*?"

"Yes. The top tier. You keep your hands off my tier. Also, when you feed me the cake, if you smear it all over my face like everyone on YouTube, I will divorce you on the spot."

He laughed again, and she couldn't believe how good it was to hear it. He hadn't sounded happy in *so long*. "Also, The Pizza Place is catering the reception."

This time he did snort. "What? I thought we were having a potluck."

"I didn't want to have a potluck."

"So we're having *pizza?* At our wedding reception? Does anyone even do that?"

"We're not having pizza. We're having salads and lobster rolls."

He groaned. She knew he would.

"You're providing the lobsters, and Kim's cooking, or her parents are. I don't really know who's cooking. Kim just said there would be cooking. And we're doing lobsters for *my* people, not the six people you're inviting. They can have the salad."

He paused. "You're joking, right? You didn't invite only six guests for my side, did you?"

"No, of course not."

"And just where is my side going to consume this salad?"

She took a deep breath. "Bill's Boat Shop."

"What?" He pushed her off him so he could look at her face. "What?" he said again.

"He's Kim's cousin, and it's the only space big enough to have tables and dancing—"

"We're going to dance? I can't dance!"

She'd been worried about his reaction, but now that he was freaking out, she was getting a perverse sort of satisfaction from it. "You're going to dance. Just one slow song. You can do it. I'll lead." She put her head back on his chest.

"Isn't his shop full of … I don't know … *boats?*"

"He said he'd clean it out for us."

"Isn't it going to smell like diesel?"

"Probably."

"I don't even think that guy likes me."

She patted his chest. "Everybody likes you, James."

Chapter 10

The smell of grilling steaks made Emily ravenous. It was a good thing she'd brought the coleslaw, because it appeared James was planning on serving steak with a side of steak. James was the kind of man who counted steak sauce as a vegetable.

"Where *are* we going to have our honeymoon, anyway?" she asked, to distract herself from her hunger.

He looked up at her quickly, concern in his eyes. "I thought we said we were going to wait till your Christmas vacation, so I don't miss any fishing."

She nodded. "We did say that. Of course. I'm just wondering where we're going."

"I have no idea. Make a list of places you'd like to go, and then we'll see what we can afford." He looked at her, and the affection in his eyes warmed her. "You want to go out with me tomorrow?"

"What?" She didn't know what he meant.

"Fishing. You want to go out for the day? You could bring a book."

"You mean like, before the sun comes up?"

He looked down at his steaks. "You don't have to. Just thought it might be nice."

She wasn't sure she wanted to, but the look on his face ... "Sure. I'd love to."

He smiled. "Perfect. My sternman just got done, and I'm not real happy about that, but now I see the silver lining."

"What do you mean he got done?" Visions of her baiting traps flashed through her mind, and her appetite vanished.

James chuckled. "Don't panic. I didn't mean I was going to try to make you do his job. I just meant that we would be alone."

Something about James's tone annoyed her. "What do you mean? You don't think I could do his job?"

James just shook his head. "Not going there."

She stewed over that for a minute, but then her curiosity stirred. "Why did he get done? I hadn't even met him yet."

"Just as well," James muttered. He didn't answer her question for a few seconds. "I fired him," he said softly, flipping a steak.

Emily gasped. "You *what*? Why?"

James shrugged. "Doesn't matter. I don't want to talk about him. I only mentioned it so that you'd know we'd be alone."

"But what are you going to do? How are you going to find another sternman?"

"I've already posted it on Facebook. I'll find one."

"But from where?"

He shrugged again. "They just crawl out of the woodwork. Don't worry. I'll find one."

He seemed so blasé about the whole thing that she stopped worrying. What did she know? Maybe it *was* easy to find help. Maybe sternmen were a dime a dozen.

"So, who are your bridesmaids?"

Ah, the old get-me-talking-about-the-wedding-so-I'll-shut-up-about-the-sternman trick. "Brides*maids* plural? I was thinking about just one—"

He looked at her wide-eyed. "You've only asked one woman?"

"Ahuh. Why?"

"Because you need at least two. I was racking my brain trying to come up with more men, because I figured you'd want a whole gaggle of hens, but I need you to have at least two."

"Why?"

"Why?" He sounded incredulous. "Because I have already asked both Brent and John. I can't have one or the other. I mean, I guess I could just have Brent, but then John would never speak to me again."

"OK."

"OK? So who else are you going to ask?"

"I don't know."

"What about Chloe?"

Emily's chest immediately warmed at the idea, but she knew it wasn't possible. "I can't ask Chloe. She's my student."

James took a swig of his Coke and leveled a gaze over the top of the can. "No, she's your niece."

Emily let that idea roll around in her head for a bit. "Really? That would work?"

"This is Piercehaven. It'll work. It probably would've worked to just ask your student. But yeah, you can definitely have your niece in your wedding."

Sometimes she loved the way the island did things. Not usually, but this time, it would work in her favor. "All right then. I'll ask her."

"Good. You'd better hurry. Now, let's eat."

"I think I should invite Thomas."

"What?"

"I felt bad about inviting Chloe to my wedding, even though she was technically on *your* list, and not inviting Thomas. And now she's going to be a bridesmaid? He's going to feel so left out."

"Thomas wants to be a bridesmaid?"

She giggled. "That's not what I meant, and you know it. But I think I should invite him."

"Thomas isn't your niece."

"I get that."

"So you're just going to invite one random student?"

"Don't be silly. I'm going to invite his whole family."

James groaned. He wasn't a fan of the Paynes.

She reached out and rubbed his hand. "Don't worry. They can sit on my side."

They'd barely finished their meals before the fireworks started. "Come on," James said, taking her hand. He led her to a lounge chair and sat in it. He reclined and stretched his long legs out in front of him. Then he gently pulled her onto his lap. She lay back on him, thinking this part was far more exciting than the light show.

The sky above them exploded in at least six different colors. "Wow," she said softly.

"Yeah, my tax dollars at work."

She elbowed him playfully. "It's beautiful."

"Yep, and so are you. I love you, Emily."

TRESPASS

"I love you too, James."

"Thanks for putting up with me."

"You bet."

They lay like that for the rest of the show. But it wasn't nearly long enough.

Chapter 11

Emily set an alarm on her almost useless cell phone. (She didn't get much use out of it with no cell service on the island and no Wi-Fi in her house. She only kept the phone around for its games and flashlight.) Then, after twenty minutes of wrestling with it, she managed to set a backup alarm on the old radio clock that had come with the house. She couldn't believe something with only three buttons could be so difficult to operate.

When they both went off at four-thirty in the morning, she wasn't sure which device to smash first. Then she decided she didn't have time for violence. James would be there in minutes, and she hadn't even drunk her daily pot of coffee yet.

She smiled as she brushed her teeth. The last time she'd gone out with James fishing, he'd proposed marriage. She wondered what he had in store this time.

TRESPASS

She had just poured her second cup of coffee when she heard his truck pull in. It was so sweet of him to come pick her up. Her house was not between his and the dock. She didn't think he'd gone to pick his sternman up every morning. But then, she'd never asked, either.

She tried to get to the door before he could get out of the truck, and in her haste, sloshed her coffee all over her arm. She cried out, in genuine grief more than physical pain, not sure if she could survive on only one cup, but she didn't want to make him wait.

When she climbed into the cab of his truck, he handed her a lidded paper cup with steam curling off the top, and she was sure she'd never loved him more. That was a gift second only to the diamond ring.

"Did you go to the bathroom?" he asked.

What am I, five? "Of course. I just got up."

"All right. Just thought I'd check. We can't just pull into a gas station when you decide you need to go."

She rolled her eyes. Sometimes he was so annoying. She loved him anyway.

"What's in the backpack?" he asked.

"Diapers."

He laughed, and the sound of it was exceptionally rewarding.

"Couple of books, and some snacks." She put the bag on the floor.

"You need more than one book?"

"I can't bring just one. What if I decide I don't like it? I've got to have a backup."

"I can't imagine putting in all the work of reading half a book and then not finishing it."

"Reading isn't work. Unless of course you're trying to finish a bad book."

Sunlight was already peeking over the horizon as he drove back down the island, toward the harbor. By the time they were in the launch, the sky was transforming into a painter's palette of pinks.

"Red sky in the morning, sailors take warning?" she said. "Is that true?"

"Everything in the Bible is true."

She made a *pfft* sound. "That's not from the Bible."

"Matthew 16," James said, a little out of breath from rowing. "Jesus said, 'When evening comes, you say, "It will be fair weather, for the sky is red," and in the morning, "Today it will be stormy, for the sky is red."' We English speakers made it rhyme, though." He laughed at his own joke. She did too.

"Any other Bible verses about lobstering?"

"Just the ones in Leviticus that tell us not to eat them."

She smiled. She thought it was so cute that he could dedicate his whole life to something when he couldn't stand to eat it.

"But didn't God later tell Peter that what was unclean was now clean?"

James grimaced. "He didn't mean lobster."

They reached Sally's mooring and pulled up alongside her.

"How many traps are we hauling today?"

"Four hundred."

She almost swallowed her tongue. *Four hundred?*

He took her hand and helped her climb aboard Sally, and she tried not to recoil at the smell of the bait. "So," he said, his tongue in his cheek, "you want to be the sternman?"

"I don't know," she said slowly. "Do I?"

"You'd better get dressed then," he said, and handed her a pair of boots and a pair of gloves. She took them gingerly, and then he held a pair of oil pants out to her. "Don't forget these." They appeared to have been special ordered for Goliath.

As James fired up the engine, she pulled the pants on over her jeans and felt like a clown. Then she put on the boots and could barely move. He began to motor away from the mooring, and she staggered sideways. This was going to be so much fun.

"Better find your sea legs," James said.

"I would, but I have no idea where they're hiding."

A seagull landed on the bow and stood staring at her. It made her feel peculiarly uncomfortable, as if the Herring gull knew something she didn't. She tried not to look at it, which wasn't easy.

James didn't say much as they headed out to their first traps, and she was able to admire the scenery—both of the ocean and of her husband-to-be—but when he pulled off the throttle to idle beside some orange and black buoys, he beckoned her over. He grabbed the line with his gaff and pulled the buoy aboard. Then he started the winch. The seagull startled and flew away. The winch pulled and pulled, and nothing seemed to be happening. Emily wondered how deep the water was beneath them, but then the winch began to whine like someone calling for help. She supposed that sound echoed the lobsters' sentiment, if, in fact, lobsters were capable of sentiment. She hoped they didn't know they were soon to be boiled alive. She figured they couldn't possibly. Any lobster who'd met that end hadn't been able to report back to his friends.

James expertly pulled the trap up onto the gunwale. "That was supposed to be your job," he said with a foolish grin, speaking loudly to be heard over the engine.

She nodded because she didn't know what else to do. He slid the trap down the gunwale and then reached to pull a second trap aboard. Then he opened both traps. He handed her a small metal device that looked a little like a martial arts weapon. He pointed to one point of it. "This is too small. If they're too small, throw them back. If not, let me have a look."

What? Was he really going to make her do this?

"You'd better get some gloves on. And grab them by the back, like this." He demonstrated.

Yes, he was expecting her to do this.

"I'm serious. Don't get your fingers anywhere near their claws. It's a long way to the emergency room on the mainland."

She put the gloves on and then, as if diffusing a bomb, slowly stuck her hand into the trap, where four ugly critters awaited their judgment day. *Yeah, maybe God didn't mean lobsters when he gave Peter that vision.* She pulled out the smallest one. It was definitely too small. She threw it back into the depths. *Hey, that was kind of fun.* She pulled out the second lobster. That's when she realized James had already completed his trap. She looked at it. It was empty, and the bait bag had been replaced. How had he done that so fast? She tried to hurry. Second one was too small too. Third one wasn't, though. She proudly handed it to James. That's when they heard screaming.

James killed the engine and traversed his small deck to look on the other side. Emily saw another lobster boat with only one person aboard. He was waving his arms at James and hollering.

James shook his head serenely and grabbed his VHF. He hailed the boat by name and then instructed the man to switch to a different channel. When he had, James asked, "What's wrong?"

A stream of profanity spilled out of the radio's mic. James held it down by his side.

Eventually, the man stopped speaking.

"What is going on?" Emily asked. None of what that man said had made any sense. And his accent was thicker than pea soup.

"He thinks I cut his lines," James said softly.

"What? What does that mean?"

TRESPASS

"Someone grabbed his buoy and cut the lines, the ropes, that attached it to his traps. So there's no way for him to get his traps off the bottom. It's a message lobstermen send every once in a while. And he thinks I'm the messenger."

Emily resisted the urge to say, "Are you?" and eyed him closely. He didn't look as if he was savoring the moment, so she figured no, he hadn't cut anything.

After a long pause, James lifted the microphone to his mouth. "It wasn't me."

Another string of profanity. Before it was finished, James reached up and flipped the VHF back to channel 16.

"Is that him? The Nautikus guy?" She already knew the answer, but wanted confirmation.

"Yep. In all his glory."

"He doesn't seem to be a very pleasant fellow."

"Pleasant fellows don't trespass into other fishermen's waters or date PeeWee Hopkin's daughter. That's the first time I've spoken to him, but I'm not surprised by his personality."

"But he called you by name."

"I'm kind of famous." James tried for a smile, but it didn't stick. "He's angry. I can understand that. Someone just cost him thousands of dollars."

"Why, how much is a trap?"

"Just one trap isn't much, but I'm guessing they cut more than just one. Plus he's got to buy new line. If they cut them all, then he's out a *lot* of cash. Plus he's going to lose money by not fishing while he tries to get more traps—*if* he tries to get more traps."

"Why wouldn't he?"

"He might decide to cut his losses and go back to where he came from. That's sort of the purpose of sending that kind of message."

Kevin came after him on channel 16 then, but James just turned the volume down.

"Whoever's angry enough to cut his traps will certainly be willing to do it again," James said.

"What is the penalty for something like that?"

"Nothing."

"What? How is that possible?"

"Because," James said, not sounding very patient, "he's in the wrong here."

"James," she said quietly, as if someone could overhear, which was of course, impossible, "do you know who cut the traps?"

James put both his hands on the helm and didn't answer her.

Chapter 12

Emily called James late Wednesday afternoon, the day after their big day on the sea. She wanted to know if he wanted to have dinner, and offered to bring something over. He hesitated before answering, but then said sure.

Wondering why he had lacked in enthusiasm, she went through the motions of making a lasagna. Every muscle in her body hurt. Even though he'd done most of the heavy lifting, she'd tried to be a big deal, and now she was paying the price.

She never wanted to see another lobster again. At her wedding reception, she planned to eat salad with her husband.

By the time she coaxed her sore legs up to his front door, wondering how her *hamstrings* got sore by hauling traps with her back and arms, she was beyond hungry. He opened the door immediately and looked a little sheepish.

Though he'd been back for a few hours, he was still in his work clothes.

"Come on in," he said, stepping back to let her pass.

As she did, she saw a man she didn't know standing in the hallway. "Em, this is Lucas, my new sternman. Lucas, this is Emily."

Why is Lucas in your house?

As if reading her mind, James explained, "Lucas is going to be staying in the guest room for a little while."

She raised an eyebrow. "You're not from the island?"

He laughed and said, "No," but he didn't tell her where he *was* from. This made her suspicious.

"That sure does smell good," Lucas said expectantly.

"I'm sure there's enough to share," James said, taking the dish from Emily's sore arms. "He's right, Em, it does smell good. Thanks for doing this." He pulled a chair away from the kitchen table for her, and she slid into it.

"So, Lucas, have you been a sternman before?"

He chuckled as though that were a foolish question, as though *of course he had.* "Yep."

Don't laugh at me like that. You can't possibly have much experience. You look like you're eighteen.

Shocking Emily, he reached across the table and took the aluminum foil off her meal.

James gave her an apologetic look and then handed them each a plate and fork. "Water, anyone?"

"You got any bottled water?" Lucas asked. "I hate the tap water on the islands. Tastes like the ocean."

Emily raised an eyebrow at her beloved. "Yeah, James, do you have any bottled water? Maybe a Perrier?" She exaggerated the French ending of the word, and Lucas gave her a perplexed look.

"Sorry, all I got is tap."

"You got any beer?"

"The only beverage I have in this house is island tap water that tastes like the ocean." James set a glass in front of her plate and one in front of his own. Then he bent to cut the lasagna.

"So, where have you worked before?" Emily asked.

"You mean as a sternman?"

Emily nodded, trying to maintain her smile.

"Oh here, there, everywhere." He slid his plate across the table to James, who gave him the first serving. "You might as well give me another one now. I know I'll be back for more."

James obliged.

Lucas took a big bite of pasta and then said, through his full mouth, "So I hear you guys are having some drama around here."

At first, Emily didn't know what he was talking about. Basketball coach drama? Windmills drama? Wedding planning drama? Then she saw the look on James's face and knew what Lucas had meant. Oh *that.*

"Not really," James said. "Just a little dustup."

"Somebody cut all that dude's traps? That's more than a dustup."

"Not all his traps. Just a few."

This was news to Emily, news she found oddly comforting. The deed was still an awful one, but more of a message than complete and utter life-destroying sabotage.

"Still, I'm sure he took off," Lucas said. "Unless he's a complete idiot, he got the message."

Emily couldn't help herself. "Do *you* know who cut his traps?"

Lucas and James exchanged a look. Then Lucas looked down at his food. "No idea."

"This is very good, honey. Thanks again."

James must have liked it, because he ate his first serving, and then a second, in record time. Emily hadn't even finished her first. Lucas was on his fourth piece when James said, "Emily and I are going to go out for a while." Then James stood and headed for the door, not even waiting to see if Emily would follow.

Which of course, she did.

She headed for the truck, but James said, "Let's take a walk." He took her hand.

"Lucas? Why is he—"

"It's a common thing," he said. "These guys are from the mainland. They won't be here long, don't want to make a big financial commitment to stay somewhere. Not that there really is anywhere to stay here anyway. He won't be here long. Just a few months."

A few months? "It's still weird," she said.

"And I'm telling you it's not." He sounded a little testy.

"So, is he going to be there on our wedding night? Just hanging around eating your food?"

"No, Brent will be hosting him that night."

"Does Brent know that?"

"Not yet."

Emily smiled up at him and leaned into him. "Where are we going?"

"How about The Big Dipper? We could go have dessert."

"Sounds good." They were almost there. She took a deep breath of the crisp night air. "Feels good to walk."

"And if we have the pecan pie, it'll be a good thing we walked."

The Big Dipper was crowded. Nary an empty barstool in the place. Brent was occupying one of them, and Emily laughed at the idea of telling him now that his wedding gift would be babysitting a sternman. But it looked like Brent was pretty serious about his drinking, so after just a manly nodded greeting from James, they passed Brent and found a corner table to claim. Then they both did order the pecan pie—a la mode even. Emily remembered her pre-wedding diet, and then decided she'd rather have pie.

The server delivered their treats, and they'd just picked up their forks when they heard a commotion by the door. Emily turned to see a man she didn't know trying to enter the bar. A man she only knew by sight was trying to stop that from happening. *What on earth?*

"That's Linville," James said.

"Nautikus guy?" she asked without looking at James. Her eyes were glued to the doorway.

"Yep."

Kevin had pushed past the one-man dam and had gotten into Brent's face, swearing again. The man sure did know how to curse. Amid all the vulgarity, Emily heard him accuse Brent of cutting his traps. At first, Brent didn't react. Then Kevin started poking him in the chest. This brought Brent off the barstool. James stood too, but didn't approach yet.

"Nobody wants you here, big shot," Brent said. "Why don't you go back home where you belong?"

Another stream of curses.

"Get out and sober up," Brent said and turned back to his beer.

Kevin pushed him. Hard. Brent fell into the bar. When he turned back around, even his ears had flushed red. Then he smiled, a weird, evil smile Emily had never seen before on gentle Brent's face.

Kevin had turned to leave, as if the men in the bar were just going to let him walk away from that. Brent, moving more quickly than Emily had ever seen him move, grabbed the back of Kevin's jeans with his right hand, and the hair on Kevin's head with his left. Then he half-pushed, half-carried Kevin to the door. Someone opened the door for him, and he threw Kevin through it, as if he was a dry stick of pulp, as if this maneuver was something they had all rehearsed multiple times.

"If I see your slimy face in here again, I'll break it," Brent hollered after him, and then punctuated his threat with a few curse words of his own.

James sat back down.

Emily watched the door for another minute to see if Kevin would return.

"He won't be back," James said.

Emily turned around. "How do you know?"

"Nobody's that stupid."

Emily pushed what was left of her pie around on her plate. "James?"

"Yeah."

"Is Brent the one who cut the traps?"

James dropped his fork. She looked at him and was surprised to see the shock on his face. "Of course not! Are you kidding?"

No, she hadn't been kidding. She'd thought it a perfectly reasonable question. "Well, why did Kevin accuse him? Why didn't—"

"How should I know? I can't read the lowlife's mind."

She began her sentence again. "Why didn't he accuse the other dozen lobstermen at the bar? Why didn't he accuse you again?"

James was glaring at her. This made her angry. Why was he mad at her?

TRESPASS

"*I'm* not accusing you of anything. I know you didn't do anything. I'm just saying, how can you be so sure of Brent's innocence? You've said yourself, the guy's no saint."

"Brent didn't cut anybody's traps," he said through clenched teeth.

"Fine." She put her fork down. "I'm done." And she got up and headed for the door.

Chapter 13

When Emily got to the gym the next day, James greeted her with an enthusiastic kiss. She wasn't sure if he was trying to pretend that nothing had happened the night before, or if in his estimation, nothing of note *had*.

Either way, she went with it and tried to return his enthusiasm, with both the kiss and then with the basketball game. The latter part wasn't, in truth, difficult. Though she was sick to death of basketball, she couldn't help but love watching her girls do their thing. It was so orchestrated, so graceful—a sweaty symphony.

In the second half, Chloe went up for a rebound and somehow got her feet knocked out from under her. She came down hard and fast and put her left hand down to break her fall. The sound that came out of that child's throat made Emily cold all over. Overwhelmed by a maternal instinct she didn't even really recognize, she had to fight herself not to leap off the bleachers and run to Chloe's side. After a quick nod from a referee, Chloe's actual mother, Gina, did just that, and Emily held her breath waiting to hear some sort of verdict.

She didn't get one. James and Gina helped Chloe up and off the floor, and then, after Gina changed Chloe's footwear—can't let the holy hightops touch actual dirt—Chloe left the gym, holding a bag of ice over her arm and still crying. It didn't look good.

As soon as she was out of sight, Emily had a thought: *She's going to be wearing a cast in my wedding.* Then she felt guilty for making Chloe's injury about her wedding. She then told herself, *At least I didn't have the thought till she was out of sight.*

At the end of the game, Emily gingerly approached James. She was starving, and wanted to go get some food with him, but didn't want a repeat of last night's argument.

She didn't make it all the way to James, though, before getting cut off by PeeWee. *Oh, now what?*

"Are you doing any summer softball?" he said quickly, harshly, without even a stab at a friendly preamble.

She didn't know what to say.

He didn't give her much time to come up with something. "You had a winning season, so you just decide to take the summer off? Why aren't you scheduling anything? There are tournaments all over the state. The Jasper girl is playing for someone else. You trying to get her to not play for us next year?"

Emily didn't know there were tournaments, didn't know Juniper Jasper was playing for someone else, and knew there was no chance Juniper would be playing for Piercehaven the next year anyway. Her dad had only moved to the island to build the windmills. The windmills were almost built.

PeeWee took a step closer to her.

She shuffled back.

"And if the Jasper girl isn't going to be pitching next year, don't you think you should be getting Hailey ready?"

She almost snickered. Hailey was a bit busy at the moment, playing basketball every minute of every day. And why did PeeWee even care? His daughter was terrible at softball.

"If you don't want to coach, just say so. If you're not going to do it, maybe I should—"

She didn't even see him coming, but her knight in shining Carhartts stepped between her and her accuser. "Enough, PeeWee."

PeeWee opened his mouth, but James didn't give him a chance to speak. "Just shut up."

Emily didn't think James told people to shut up, but if anyone deserved it ...

James lowered his voice. "Feeling bad about yourself because of this giant mess you've created? So you needed to find someone to pick on?" James crept closer to him as he spoke. "I don't want you talking to my wife again, *ever*. I don't care if you're king of the school board. Now get out of my gym and go get your daughter and her spineless boyfriend under control."

PeeWee's face was on fire. Emily thought he might punch James, but he would have to reach up some distance to do so, so maybe he thought that would attract more attention than it was worth. Amazingly, after a few tense seconds, PeeWee simply turned and stomped away. Emily couldn't believe what she'd just witnessed. So many odd things: She didn't think James spoke to anyone like that; She didn't think PeeWee backed down from anyone; and James had called her *his wife*. As annoyed as she could have been with any part of the situation she'd just been a part of (the rudeness, the implied chauvinism, the possessiveness), she was delighted. He called her his wife. Even though they weren't married yet. So he considered her his wife already. He really wanted to marry her.

James was staring at her. She tried to smile, and then realized she was already grinning foolishly.

"Sorry about that," James said. "He's out of his mind."

She just nodded.

"Want to go down to the clinic, check on Chloe?"

"Of course."

In the truck, James told her that Kevin had gone out on the water again, and that this time, *all* of his traps had been cut. James relayed the information without emotion, and Emily had no idea how he felt about this development. Concerned? Guilty? Joyful? Satisfied?

"Do you think he'll give up now?"

"I sure hope so." He paused, thoughtful. "He'll at least have to pause. He's going to have to go to the mainland to get more traps. No one on the island is going to sell him any … unless PeeWee is foolish enough to give him some, but I don't know if he has any extras, and I doubt even PeeWee is crazy enough to give up his own traps." He paused again. "I don't know, Em. I just can't believe how stupid the guy is. I mean, how is any of this worth it? What's he trying to prove? We're not going to stop. We're not going to suddenly say, 'OK, sure, go ahead and steal our waters.'"

We. He'd said *we*. Emily shuddered. Just how tangled in all this was her husband-to-be?

Gina and Chloe weren't in the waiting room of the clinic. James asked the woman behind the glass for details, which, illegal or not to do so, she gladly provided. Chloe was in having X-rays. It was probably broken. They would know soon. They'd called the doctor in.

James and Emily settled into the hard plastic chairs to wait.

Emily eyed the snack machine across the room. "Mmmm, how about a PayDay?"

James nodded and stood to fetch some snacks.

"Hang on, James," the woman behind the glass said. "I've got a key to the machine."

Three PayDays later, Emily was no longer starving. She was sick. But Chloe was in the waiting room, her eyes red but dry, and a fresh cast on her arm.

"Hi, honey." Emily gave her a hug, taking care to avoid the cradled arm.

"You guys didn't have to come," Gina said.

"Where's John?" James asked.

"He's on the mainland. Coming back on the last ferry. Should be here any second."

"So I have a question for you, Chloe. Would you be my bridesmaid?"

Her red eyes lit up. "Really?"

"Yeah. Really." Emily wondered how she ever could have doubted the idea.

She looked at her mom. "Can I?"

Gina nodded. Her eyes looked a little wet too all of a sudden.

"Yeah! Of course!" Chloe hugged Emily again. "When do I get my dress?"

Emily couldn't sleep. She was worried about Kevin Linville. She was worried about Chloe. She was worried about their church situation. And she was angry that she couldn't stop going over and over her PeeWee confrontation. She kept thinking of clever things she could have said, things she *wished* she'd said.

Finally, after two hours of her mind racing around a hamster wheel, she got out of bed and onto her knees.

At first, she just rested there, trying to clear her brain out. Then she prayed, "Father, what a mess. Please help me to stop thinking about PeeWee. Am I supposed to be doing summer softball? The thought never occurred to me, and I don't even think I could field a team, with so many girls playing basketball. If I *am* supposed to be doing something with softball, could you make that clear? And please don't let me lose that job. As you know, I *love* coaching softball." She paused, trying to organize her thoughts. Then she decided she didn't need to do that for God. "God, I'm supposed to marry James, right? He's acting so strangely. I love him so much, and I know he loves you. Maybe you could help him out with … no, I *know* you are helping him. Thank you for helping him out with all the stuff he's dealing with. I don't know if he's right about this church thing … is he, God? I think it would be nice to have a real church to raise children in, but what he says makes sense … I don't know … but give him guidance there, and please don't let our church fall apart over this. Is he right that you don't want us to have a church building? That seems so strange." She paused, hoping God would answer her. "Do you want us to have church in our living room?" And then a feeling overwhelmed her. It came out of nowhere, and was so strong that she thought it had to have come from God: *Support James.* "Uh … was that you, God?" She knew it had been. "OK, I will support him.

ROBIN MERRILL

I can do that. Thank you, God. Thank you for everything, and please help me to fall asleep. And thank you that I don't have to get up in the morning. In Jesus' name—oh wait, one more thing. Please protect the people of this island from Kevin Linville. And please protect Kevin Linville from the people of this island. Actually, please just make him go home."

Chapter 14

Emily was so excited to meet Kim for dinner and wedding planning, she almost forgot to feed her cats. One of them, Daisy Buchanan, howled at her when she reached for the door handle. So she put down her tote of wedding stuff, took care of business, and still made it out the door in plenty of time.

At least it would've been in time, had she not gotten stuck behind an "island car" that was rolling about five miles per hour down the road. Technically, all cars in the State of Maine had to have a yearly inspection, to prove they were road-safe, including those cars on Piercehaven. But if a car never left the island, well, no cop was going to pull that car over for black smoke flowing out the exhaust (as in this case) and rusted floorboards (she was making an assumption). She kept looking beneath the car to see if the operator was using his feet Flintstone style.

Finally, she rolled into the small parking lot of The Pizza Place.

Kim was waiting for her at a table and looked up as she approached. "Hiya, want something to eat?"

"Do you have to make it?"

Kim's brow furrowed in confusion.

"I don't want you to have to scurry off to the kitchen to make me—"

"Oh no, I can have Dad do it. It's Friday night, all hands on deck."

Emily looked around the empty restaurant.

"Most people carry out."

"Ah." Emily slid into the booth. "I would love a salad."

Kim snickered. "No pizza?"

"Not till after August 5."

"Okeedoke." Kim stood up. "Why'd you pick August anyway?"

Emily shrugged. "I was in a hurry. Seemed like the soonest we could pull a wedding together. Which, we would have failed at if not for you."

Kim smiled. "Nah, I'm not doing much at all. You want any meat on your salad?"

Emily raised an eyebrow. "Does a pepperoni salad count as healthy?"

"I don't think so. How about tuna?"

Emily resigned herself to that suggestion and began to unpack her tote. She couldn't believe how much stuff she'd accumulated in just three months of wedding planning. And Kim had even more stuff piled on the table.

Kim returned and slid into her spot. "OK, where are we at?"

"I brought the invitations."

"Good grief, those should've been mailed months ago."

"I know, I know." Emily hung her head in embarrassment. "So what do you think about making Chloe a bridesmaid?"

Kim's eyebrows flew up. "Chloe? Sure? Instead of Naomi or in addition to her?"

"In addition to her. James wanted to have two groomsmen."

"Sure. OK. You, me, Chloe, and Naomi need to go dress shopping. Let's go to Portland—"

"I was thinking about ordering a dress online."

"Don't be ridiculous. We're going to Portland. I promised Dad I would work tomorrow, but how about Sunday?"

"After church?"

Kim scrunched up her nose. "Nah, we'll want to get on the first ferry. How about Monday?"

"I'm pretty sure Naomi works every weekday. How about next Saturday?"

Kim wrote something in her notebook. "Next Saturday it is. You make sure Naomi and Chloe can come, and I'll make an appointment."

"You have to make an appointment to go dress shopping?"

Kim gave her a condescending look. "Only if you want a dressing room." She took half of the invitations off the stack.

"I've already addressed them," Emily said, thinking that's what Kim meant to do. "But I didn't seal them, because I wasn't sure what to put on the RSVP card. Do they need to RSVP? And how? Online? Am I supposed to buy another seventy stamps for the stupid little RSVP cards?"

"Well, it's super cheap of you to ask them to send the card and *not* buy a stamp for them, and I doubt many of them would even mail it back." She looked up quickly. "Sorry, maybe your family is more polite. None of my relatives would buy a stamp for me."

Emily laughed. "No, your assumption is fairly accurate."

"So let's just ask them to call or text their RSVP. Does that work?"

"Perfect."

They began the slow work of handwriting the RSVP instructions on the little cards. Emily's salad arrived, and she began to multitask, only dropping a chunk of juicy tomato on one invitation before Kim said, "Just eat. I'll finish these."

Between bites, Emily said, "I didn't see James today. Do you know if Kevin was out on the water?"

Kim didn't look up. "You mean Harley's boyfriend?"

"Yeah."

"Caleb said he wasn't. Or at least he didn't see him. But I think he might have been at some point. Because someone cut all of Brent's lines."

Emily stopped chewing. She swallowed hard. "You're kidding." She felt sick to her stomach thinking about how much that would cost Brent and his family. Brent usually had eight hundred traps in the water. "But Brent's not the one who cut Kevin's lines."

Kim looked up at her without lifting her head, so her expression was eerie. "OK," she said, her voice dripping with irony.

"What? He didn't!" Emily wasn't even sure if this was true, and wasn't sure why she was defending him with such oomph.

Kim looked back down. "I really don't know who cut them, and I don't care. I just want the guy to go away."

"My thoughts exactly."

"So, I can't believe you got James to agree to a wedding during fishing season. How long will your honeymoon be?"

"How long?"

"Yeah, how many days will you be away? Is he going to have someone fish his traps for him?"

Emily laughed. "Oh no, he may love me enough to marry me during fishing season, but not enough to honeymoon with me during fishing season. We're planning to go somewhere, not sure where yet, during Christmas break, when I have time off from school."

Kim's brow furrowed again. "But isn't that basketball season?"

Huh. Emily hadn't thought of that. "I guess we won't be going away for very many days then." She took a drink of her water and then laughed. "Or maybe we're honeymooning in Bingham, or Rangeley, or Jackson, or some other exotic location where there's a Maine class D high school."

Kim tittered, and then gave Emily a sarcastic smirk. "Or maybe you'll get to honeymoon on Vinalhaven. That would be a real change of pace."

Chapter 15

Despite Searsport's class C status, the Piercehaven Panthers were wiping the floor with them. Emily had learned that, with Maine basketball, the size of the school meant much less than one might think. Hailey Leadbetter would be a star on any team, from any school of any size—Emily was sure of it. Right now, she already had twenty points, and it was still the first half.

Emily was excited to see what she picked for a college and was already wondering how the Panthers would fare without her. She was heading into her senior year, and though there were several talented juniors and sophomores, there wasn't another Hailey. Emily wondered if there ever would be.

Chloe sat sulking on the bench, holding her cast in her hand. It was already covered with Sharpie signatures, and Emily marveled at the facts: that is a weird tradition; and that is a timeless tradition. When someone moved to go into the game, Emily slid down the bench to be next to Chloe and rubbed her back. "It will heal."

"I know. I just hate just sitting here."

"I know. But at least it didn't happen during basketball season."

Chloe looked at her as though she were stupid, an expression Chloe delivered to her frequently. "Basketball players are made in the summertime, Miss Morse."

Emily snickered. "Did you get that off a T-shirt?"

Now Chloe's expression said, "Are you crazy?"

Emily thought the proverb probably came from her former basketball coach, and let it go.

James seemed more relaxed than she'd seen him in the past few weeks. He was even joking around with the girls on the bench. And when the ref called Hannah for her fourth foul when she was ten feet away from anyone on the opposite team, he didn't even flinch. She wondered if his good mood was a reflection of the fact that Kevin Linville had gone home.

She got her chance to ask after the game. "Any sign of the trespassing lobsterman?"

He completely ignored her. "Can you take a few extra girls tonight?"

"What? Why?"

"One of our hosts is sick."

"Where am I supposed to put them? I've only got one pull out couch. It's a squeeze just to get two girls comfy on it."

James moved his lips to one side of his face. Emily thought this meant he was deep in thought, but it was also a hilarious expression. She tried not to laugh at him.

"I'd offer to switch houses with you for the night," he said, "but … the sternman."

"Yeah. The sternman. What about Abe and Lily?"

He nodded and sighed. "Yeah, I just feel bad because I ask them for so much."

"Well, desperate times."

"Yeah, desperate times. All right. I'll go call them."

She waited around for him to return, and by the time he did, the Searsport girls were all out of the locker room and standing around waiting for their sleeping assignments. A few of them were already in their pajamas, which Emily thought was cute. They'd done this before.

James matched people up, Lily showed up in record time to retrieve her guests, and soon all that was left was Emily's two guests. But she couldn't stand not getting an answer to her question. She leaned toward James conspiratorially. "Well?"

"Well what?"

"Have you seen Kevin lately?"

"Who?" He had actually forgotten about the man.

"Kevin Linville … Nautikus guy? A week ago he was all anyone could talk—"

He curled his lip. "I think he got the message when he had no traps left. No one has seen him since."

"So"—she lowered her voice—"then who cut Brent's traps?"

James smirked, apparently amused by her lobsterman-drama craving. "I think it was him trying to have the last word—right before he turned tail and ran. But, Brent says it's a price he's willing to pay to get rid of him."

Emily couldn't believe Brent would be willing to invest *thousands* of dollars to get rid of a pest, but she didn't argue the point. "So who *did* cut Kevin's traps? If it wasn't Brent. Now that it's all over, you can tell me."

James looked at the two girls standing sheepishly beside them. "You should get these girls to your house. I bet they're hungry."

Emily gave up. "OK. But we're not going to my house. I'm taking them out for pizza and a movie."

TRESPASS

"A movie?" James said, as if that was the most absurd thing he'd ever heard.

"Yeah. At Kim's apartment. She's my island hosting ace in the hole."

Chapter 16

Emily drove to the ferry with coffee in hand. She was excited to get a wedding dress. She was not excited to ride the ferry for ninety minutes, and then drive two hours to South Portland to then try on a gazillion dresses in front of an audience—one member of which was her sixteen-year-old student. She didn't understand why she couldn't just order a dress online. This *was* the twenty-first century. But, Kim was in charge.

She was excited to see her bestie of all besties—Naomi. They'd been friends since the summer before seventh grade, when they met at the annual Moxie Festival. Though they grew up in neighboring towns, they hadn't known each other till each of their families had traveled to Lisbon Falls to celebrate the best beverage known to humankind.

Emily's dad and Naomi's dad were long lost friends who reconnected at the pancake breakfast; then the girls had spent the day together: racing in the kids' fun run; watching the Moxie parade; eating Moxie ice cream out of stale cones; watching the Moxie chugging contest; and ending with the Moxie lobster dinner. If she had known then the role those little red critters would play in her future … the ferry worker in the fluorescent vest was waving to her impatiently. Shaking her brain out of its reverie, she started her car and began the slow drive down the plank.

As usual, the man on the ferry instructed her to drive into a spot she knew she couldn't possibly fit in; she did it anyway, and as always, there was room. Loading the Piercehaven ferry always defied the laws of geometry. She opened the door the eight inches she could without banging into the fifty-thousand-dollar truck beside her, and then squeezed herself out, suddenly having an overpowering hankering for an ice cold Moxie. Or even a warm one.

Kim and Chloe were already in the cabin. "Want to go up above?" Emily asked.

"Sure." Kim stood up.

So did Chloe, looking incredibly excited.

"I've been thinking," Emily said as they went up the ladderway.

"No. You are not ordering a dress on eBay."

Emily laughed. They spilled out onto the upper deck, into the brilliant early morning sunshine and ocean breeze. Emily pushed her hair behind her ears, but the wind just pulled it back out. "No. Not that. I was wondering if we could get some cases of Moxie. I would like to serve it at the reception."

Kim raised an eyebrow. "Well, that's bizarre, but sure. Why not?"

"Mmm … Moxie," Chloe said dreamily.

Emily looked at Kim. "See? It's a great idea."

They stayed topside until they were pulling into Camden harbor. It was the same scenery every trip, but Emily never tired of it. She couldn't wait for her family to see and experience her new home—and the voyage to get there.

They slid into her car and began the slow summer drive to Brunswick, where they could finally get on the highway. Until then, it would be a tourist-clogged slog down Route 1, slamming on the brakes for every art gallery, lobster shack, farmer's market, antique store, and lawn sale along the way. They saw as many out-of-state plates as Maine ones.

After one particularly hairy near-collision, when they came around a sharp corner to see a line of cars pulling into a fudge store, Kim said, "Thank God the tourists don't come to Piercehaven. I don't think I could take it."

She pulled around the cars, noticing the line of children waiting to have their picture taken with their faces poking out through a plywood moose's head. "I don't know," Emily said, thinking of her nonexistent school budget. "They bring a lot of money with them."

"I don't care," Kim said emphatically. "Not worth it."

Emily thought Chloe was being awfully quiet, and was just about to ask her if she was OK. She adjusted her rear view mirror so she could see her, and then noticed she had earbuds in. Never mind. She put the rear view back on the road.

Finally, they made it to I-95, Maine's only interstate, and finally, that interstate spat them out onto the Maine Mall Road, where Kim directed Emily to Jacqueline's Bridal Boutique. The place was huge. As Emily climbed out of the car, she looked up at it uneasily. She thought it looked a little out of her budget. "I don't know," she said slowly.

Kim got out of the car. "What? Did you want to go to Hussey's?"

Emily frowned. She didn't understand. Did Kim just call her a hussy? "What?"

Kim looked at her, her eyes full of light. "You know, *Hussey's General Store?* In Windsor. They sell beer, bait, pizza, guns, and wedding dresses." She made air quotes with her fingers. "If they ain't got it, you don't need it."

Emily slammed her car door. "You're kidding."

Kim stopped walking and stared at her. "How do you *not* know about Hussey's? The place is a legend."

"Sorry," Emily said. "My brain spends most of its free time in stories, and I've never read a novel about a store called Hussey's."

"Well, then, consider this your education. It's the store of all stores. People even get their wedding pictures taken in front of the gasoline signs. Obviously, you need to get off the island more," Kim said, and then all three of them laughed at that all the way into the store.

The air conditioning hit them like a tidal wave, taking Emily's breath away.

A woman in a suit-dress and lots of makeup met them before they could get too far into the store. "Good morning! Welcome to Jacqueline's Bridal Boutique! Do you have an appointment?" Her pretension was so thick Emily was surprised she wasn't choking on it.

"We do," Kim said. "For Kim Aronson."

"Oh, OK." She stuck out her hand. "And you are?"

"Kim Aronson," Kim deadpanned.

"And are you the bride?"

Oh my soul, Emily thought, *can we just go look around?*

"I am not. This is the bride, Emily. This is a bridesmaid, Chloe. Another bridesmaid is meeting us here shortly, and we'd like to get started, as we have to catch a ferry."

"Oh! How exciting!" She shook Emily's and Chloe's hands. "My name is Erica, and I will be helping you today. Are you from Peaks Island?"

Kim looked horrified. Peaks Island was part of the city of Portland, only about a mile off the mainland. Emily knew that her islanders didn't even consider it a real island. "Uh, no," Kim said. "Don't their ferries run till midnight? Why would they be in a hurry? We're from Piercehaven. Can we start looking around?"

"Sure, follow me!" The woman, still fake-smiling, turned and led them into the bowels of bridery.

"I still can't believe we needed an appointment," Emily muttered to Kim.

"It's a thing. You need one at Hussey's too," Kim whispered back.

122

Erica finally stopped, pointing to a dress on a headless mannequin. "This is our newest dress, and the design is *so sleek*, I'm just crazy about it."

Emily thought it was hideous; it looked as though someone *really* had to use up all the fabric in the dress factory, but she tried to keep an open mind. She scanned the dress for a price, didn't see any, then looked at the other dresses, the ones hanging on racks, and saw that those did have tags. "Just out of curiosity, how much does that dress cost?"

"Fourteen ninety-five."

Chloe gasped.

Erica read the situation and didn't even try to hide her disappointment. "And what is your budget limitation?"

Emily was suddenly very embarrassed to say.

"We don't have any limitations," Kim said, "but we're looking for something a bit more traditional. Can we look around? We'll find you if we need you."

Erica looked as though she had been forced to swallow something sour, but then nodded and disappeared.

Thank the heavens.

"You said two hundred dollars, right?" Kim muttered.

"I did, but is that even possible?"

"Absolutely. Follow me."

Even bridal boutiques have a clearance section. Kim started pulling out dresses and handing them to Chloe.

"Is there something wrong with these?" Emily asked. "Why are they in clearance? Did women get married with the tags on and then return them?"

Kim laughed. "No. They're just last year's styles. They're fine, and I'll go over the one you pick with a fine-toothed comb to make sure it's perfect."

For the thousandth time, Emily thanked God for Kim.

"There's my blushing bride!" a voice squealed from behind them, and Emily turned to see Naomi rushing at her with arms wide.

Soon those arms were tight around her, and Emily realized just how much she'd missed her friend.

"Thanks so much for coming," Emily said.

"Are you kidding? I wouldn't miss this for the world."

Chapter 17

Emily tried on six dresses before she was ready to quit. She was exhausted. She was frustrated. The first dress made her look chubby. The next two made her look like an old lady. The next one was barely a dress at all—she might as well walk down the aisle naked. The next one was so scratchy she couldn't get it off fast enough. The sixth dress—back to chubby. "I don't think I can do this anymore," she said from inside the dressing room. It wasn't fair. Her bridesmaids and wedding planner got to sit on a leather couch and drink sparkling water from champagne glasses.

"We need to see that one!" Kim called out.

"No, you really don't." Emily pushed it down over her hips. She wasn't strong enough to lift all the pearls and sequins over her head.

A granola bar slid under her door. "Here. Eat something."

Emily snatched it up. *Ah, Naomi, you know me so well.* She polished it off in three bites, and then stood chewing, looking at her next foe hanging on the hook.

Resigned, she slid it on over her head and stepped out into the spotlight. The three women, who had been chatting, fell silent.

"Whoa," Naomi said.

"That's the one," Kim said.

Emily turned toward the three-way mirrors. "Really?"

"I think it really is, Miss Morse. You look beautiful."

She had to admit—she did look fetching. The A-line clung to her waist and made it look tiny. The skirt poofed out just enough to make her look like a princess instead of a clown. The bodice had a V-neck, but not an indecent one, and the cap sleeves were made of lace— perfectly straddling the line between showing enough skin and showing too much. Here it was. *This is the one.*

Uh-oh. She hadn't looked at the price tag. And she couldn't see it now. She hurried back into her closet and stripped out of it, and then looked at the tag. Twelve hundred dollars marked down to 199. She smiled. Then she cried a little. She cried because she loved the dress. She cried because she couldn't wait to get married, and now it was really going to happen. She cried because she could afford the perfect dress. And she cried because now she could go sit on the leather couch and bark orders at her bridesmaids.

She put her normal clothes back on, realizing she'd never truly appreciated how comfortable they were, wiped her eyes, and then carried her winning dress out into the light. She nodded, and the tears came again. "You are right. This is the one."

Kim jumped up, gave her an emphatic hug, and then turned and clapped her hands. "All right, bridesmaids, get to work." Then she raised her voice. "Erica! We need another glass of bubbly over hee-ah!"

Emily collapsed gratefully on the couch. Chloe looked down at her. "Don't you want to pick out our dresses?"

Emily shook her head. "Nope. If you guys can agree, you can wear whatever you want. But you've got a two hundred dollar limit."

"Em, you are not buying my dress," Naomi said.

"Oh yes, I am, so stay within the budget."

A different suit-dress-wearing woman handed Emily a beverage. Apparently, Erica had had enough of them. Emily thanked her and looked at Naomi. "What's wrong?"

"Chloe here says that our wedding colors are red and white?"

Emily nodded as she took a sip. She swallowed. "That's right. Why? You don't like red?"

"Em, *no one* has a red and white wedding."

"Naomi, welcome to the island. Now go grab every red dress and start trying them on. I'm ready for the show."

It turned out that they didn't need to grab every red dress. Chloe nailed it on the first try. Sleeveless, floor-length, A-line with a V-neck, with a silk sash around the waist. Not only did they look absolutely gorgeous, but the dresses also coordinated with Emily's perfectly—as if the whole thing was meant to be, as if God even cared about wedding apparel.

Emily put her empty glass down, stood up from the comfy couch, and began to applaud. "Good job, ladies. You look perfect."

Chloe looked down at the tag. "It says Apple Red, but I think it's the perfect Panther Red myself."

Naomi's brow furrowed in confusion.

Emily laughed. "Yes. Like I said, they're perfect."

Erica reappeared to secure her commission, though it would certainly be less than she'd hoped. She managed to sell them all shoes and Emily a small tiara, but that's where they drew the line. Erica couldn't believe Emily was going to go sans veil, but Emily stuck to her guns.

"All right. Why don't you put the dress back on, and our seamstress will take the measurements for your alterations?"

Kim physically stepped between Emily and the vulture. "No thanks. We have someone on the island who is going to do that. For free."

On the way out to the car, Emily said, "Do we really need alterations? I thought everything fit fine."

"We need to see you in the dress and the shoes at the same time. Then we can adjust to make the gown the perfect length. Same thing for the bridesmaids. We need to make sure their dresses are the same length. They'll look ridiculous if Naomi's is longer than Chloe's.

Emily thought "ridiculous" might be an exaggeration. "Who is doing the alterations?"

"Don't know yet, but I'll find someone. Things on the island just have a way of working themselves out."

Chapter 18

Sunday morning delivered a joyous surprise. Emily didn't recognize him at first, but James identified the newcomer as Kim's husband, Greg. At first, he stood near the back, but James got up, went and talked to him for a bit, and then brought him back to sit in their row of folding chairs. Emily thought, *Too bad we don't have donuts and coffee for guests, like at a real church.* Then she realized that she could probably manage to serve donuts and coffee just about anywhere.

Up close, Greg didn't look as though he felt well. His skin was dark and leathery like the rest of the lobstermen, but beyond that, his face and eyes looked red, and he appeared to be exhausted. He sure did seem to be a quiet man. He was silent through the singing, stayed rooted to his spot during the greeting, and sat somberly throughout the sermon.

At the end of the service, Abe got up to close in prayer, but then he just stood there, staring at the floor in front of him. Just as Emily was wondering if he was all right, he looked up. "I think someone here needs prayer." He paused again. "I don't want to embarrass anyone, but if you're here right now and you're in trouble, if you know you can't do this on your own, and you need God, I'm inviting you right now to come down here and stand beside me. I just want to pray for you. *We* just want to pray for you."

At first, no one moved. Most people looked around nosily, Emily being one of them. The pause grew, and Emily looked at Abe, trying to will him to give up. *No one's coming down front, Abe. Let's get this show on the road.* It was approximately 110 degrees in the room.

As if responding directly to Emily's silent plea, Abe said, "Sorry, friends. The Holy Spirit is telling me to be patient. Someone here is hurting."

At that, Greg stood up. He looked at Abe, nodded, and then began to make his way toward the front. A sob sounded to Emily's right, and she looked to see that Kim had stood too.

"Anyone who wants to, come and help me pray for our friend here," Abe said. Then he lay a hand on Greg's shoulder and began to pray. James got there and lay a hand on

Greg's other shoulder. Soon Greg was surrounded. Those who couldn't touch him held a hand out in his direction. Kim took Caleb's hand and led him to the front. Somehow, Abe knew when she approached because he paused his prayer and said, "Can you guys part right there and let Kim and Caleb through?" Abe finished his prayer, and then James began to pray, in his deep, steady voice. As he prayed, Greg let out a sob.

"Greg," James said, more softly, "do you know Jesus personally?"

Emily didn't hear Greg's response.

James said, "Do you want to?"

This time, she heard his response: "I just want my family back."

"I can imagine," James said, and Emily was amazed by the compassion in his voice. "And Jesus can make that happen, but right now this isn't about your family. This is about *you*. This is about the fact that you were created to walk hand-in-hand with the one who created you. But you've got to admit that you need him. You've got to *want* that connection, that relationship."

At first, nothing, but then Greg let out a shaky, "I do."

"Great, Greg. That's great. All you have to do is pray, and ask Jesus to take over your life. Give your heart to him right now." As James led Greg in prayer, Emily prayed a prayer of her own, thanking God for bringing such an amazing godly man into her life. She couldn't believe she was going to get to marry him.

The crowd up front began to disperse, though there was still lots of crying and hugging. The worship leader began to sing "How He Loves Us" and many people joined in. At the beauty of that sound, Emily's tears joined the rest. Suddenly she wasn't in such a hurry to get out of there. It was a good thing too, because Abe made an announcement.

"Thanks for coming, everyone. We're going to vote on the building in a minute here, so if you want to vote, stick around."

Everyone under the age of eighteen went up the stairs. James walked Greg and his family out, as everyone else found their way to their seats. Emily was a little nervous that they were going to vote without James.

"OK, so you all know that I didn't want to do this," Abe began. "I think it's frankly ridiculous that we can't all reach an agreement simply through prayer and seeking God. If we were all listening to the Holy Spirit, he would have made this decision for us already, but apparently that's not going to happen. And some of you have been urging me to just do the vote, so we don't drag this debate out any longer. So we're going to vote. But I beg you, no matter how this turns out, we're still the body of Christ, and we still need to behave like followers of Jesus. People on this island are watching us. They're just waiting for us to mess up so they can ignore our message. If they catch us bickering, our testimony quickly loses power. So ..." He took a deep breath and looked around the room. "Our choices are A) begin the process of acquiring land and building a church building or B) half of us move to James's house next Sunday, and half of us stay here, and we all just keep doing what we're doing in two separate homes." He took another deep breath. Emily felt sorry for him. She glanced for the thousandth time at the stairs for James, but he was still off being wonderful with the Aronson family.

"Ready?" Abe asked. Then, "All in favor of pursuing a building project, please raise your hand." Scott and his wife raised their hands, although Scott's wife didn't look completely convinced. A few others raised their hands. The tension was palpable.

Abe didn't even appear to be counting. "OK, all in favor of multiplying this group into two groups, please raise your hand."

Support James, Emily thought as she raised her hand.

The room filled with raised hands.

She didn't look at Scott. She didn't want to see his anger.

"All right," Abe said, "I'm pretty sure that settles it. If you live closer to me, you're welcome here next Sunday at ten. If you live closer to James, you're welcome there at ten. If you live in the middle, I guess you'll have to cast lots."

Emily realized then that she would need to stock up on donuts and coffee.

There was no more fighting. People quietly and seemingly amicably left the house. James was still talking to the Aronsons, who looked ... *lighter* somehow. Emily approached and slipped her arm around James's waist. She gave Kim a huge smile, which apparently wasn't enough, because Kim gave her a bearhug. "I think it's all going to be OK," she whispered into her ear.

"I think you're right," Emily whispered back. Emily felt guilty then that she hadn't done a better job of praying for this family. But someone must have been picking up her slack. She looked up at James, wondering if it was him.

TRESPASS

Eventually, the Aronsons drove off, in two separate vehicles, but heading in the same direction this time.

James put his arm around Emily's shoulder, and she smiled up at her favorite person in the world. "The vote went your way. Church at your house on Sunday."

James squeezed her shoulder. "Good. The vote went *God's* way, you mean."

Support James. "You don't seem surprised."

"I'm not." He kissed her. "Since I've been told we're serving Moxie at our wedding, not much surprises me anymore."

Chapter 19

Emily awoke suddenly and completely. Her heart was racing, her senses on high alert. What had just woken her? She looked around her silent loft bedroom, straining her ears, but there was nothing. But there *had* been something, hadn't there? Some noise that didn't belong, some noise that would explain her current heart rate. Maybe she'd just had a bad dream? If so, that would be unusual. She tried to be stealthy as she sat up and slid her bare feet to the cool wooden floor. It was almost *too* quiet. She stood and, cringing at the deafening creaks from the bedsprings and the floor, tiptoed over to her spiral staircase and peeked downstairs.

Nick Carraway sat at the bottom looking up at her. She smiled, let out a puff of air she didn't know she'd been holding, and decided that whatever the noise had been, if there even *had* been a noise, it was nothing to worry about.

TRESPASS

She padded downstairs, stooped to swoop Nick up into her arms, and smothered him in kisses on her way to the coffee pot.

Still, as she stood looking out her kitchen window waiting for her morning elixir to drip, then as she sipped it while trying to focus on her morning devotion, and as she took a long shower, and as she got dressed, she couldn't shake this unease that something was terribly wrong. As she put on her mascara, she prayed, "Whatever is wrong with me, make it stop. Please fill me with your peace," but precious little peace arrived.

It was a long, mostly fruitless day, and when she saw James at 4:30, an unexpected wave of relief flowed over her. She didn't realize she'd been worried about him until he was in her arms.

But something was wrong with him too. He was stiff and pulled away from her early.

"You OK?"

"Yeah, of course." He looked at the floor.

"How was your day?"

"My day is always the same. Water, traps, bugs." He took a drink from his water bottle, still not looking at her.

"OK, well, you're just acting kind of upset."

He turned to the fridge to get more water. "I'm fine, Emily. Just tired. Lucas took the day off today."

"A day off? A sternman can do that?"

James shrugged. "Sternmen can do whatever they want. They often get fired, but …" His voice trailed off.

"Are you going to fire Lucas?" Emily actually felt hopeful, but then felt guilty about it.

"Not for just one day off. He's one of the best I've had. Great worker. When he's there."

She found this hard to believe, but she dropped it. She was just so relieved that James was there in front of her in one piece. She didn't really believe in premonitions, but she'd had such a weird day.

"I've got to shower and change, get ready for the game."

She watched him walk away, knowing for certain that something was really wrong, but not knowing what, if anything, she should do about it. Then she tried to get comfortable on the couch, and she waited. She wished they didn't have a game that day. She was sick of basketball. She missed softball. Maybe PeeWee was right. (Now *there's* a thought she didn't often think.) Maybe they *should* have some sort of summer softball.

TRESPASS

James reappeared looking cleaner but no happier. He sat down beside her to dress his feet. She put a hand on his back, and he flinched beneath her touch. She jerked her hand away. *What on earth?*

"You want to ride with me?" he said quickly.

"Sure."

They were silent as they left the house, drove to the school, and walked into the gym. But soon the sounds of bouncing balls, giggling girls, and squeaking sneakers filled the vacuum. Emily sat, resigning herself to just do her job as statistician. She could psychoanalyze the love of her life later.

But it didn't quite work out that way, because James's behavior only grew stranger. When Sydney cussed out Victoria, he didn't correct her. *Like father like daughter,* Emily thought, glancing at PeeWee in the bleachers. When Zoe hit three three-pointers in a row, in less than a minute, he didn't even seem to notice. And when Camden Christian went to a zone defense, he didn't adjust their offense, which even Emily knew didn't make sense. After a few trips down the floor, Hailey just switched the offense herself, a move which, on a normal day, would have incensed her coach, but he didn't even blink.

Is he nervous about the wedding? No, he's not. This has nothing to do with the wedding. Stop making everything about you. Then suddenly she knew what it was about: Kevin Linville. He was back. Something had happened. Had he cut *James's* traps? That would explain everything.

The game took forever, and Emily wished basketball had a mercy rule like softball. Losing by a hundred points? Just hit the showers. But alas, there was no mercy in store for the Camden Christian Conquerors, and the clock slowly ticked down while Hailey piled insult atop injury. Again, it was weird that James still had her in the game. He would normally be playing the younger players by now, but he just stood there, arms across his chest, watching the ball go back and forth.

Finally, the blessed buzzer sounded. She waited for him to give some last words to his girls, and then watched them line up and high five the defeated Conquerors. When the Panthers dispersed, she approached. "You want to get some dinner?"

He looked at her, and he did indeed look tired. "You know what? I don't feel well. I'm sorry, but I think I'm just going to go home and go to bed."

TRESPASS

"Oh ... OK ... you want me to bring you some soup?" She knew it sounded lame even as she said it, but she was panicking a little.

"Emily, I love you, but really ... I just need ... I don't need anything." He stepped away from her to return a ball to the bin, but then, like an afterthought, he came back and kissed her on the top of the head. "I love you. Everything is fine."

But everything most certainly wasn't fine. Not even close.

Chapter 20

Emily woke to birds singing out her window and the feeling that an enormous weight had been lifted from her chest. Whatever yesterday was, it was over. God's mercies are new every morning.

She flitted down the stairs, a foolish grin on her face. Nick looked up at her, alarmed, and then dodged her morning embrace. Her smile stayed in place, however, until she opened the fridge to see that she was out of coffee creamer. Then the smile vanished, replaced with jaw-dropped horror. She looked at the coffee pot, which was already percolating. She looked down at her pajamas and bare feet. She was certainly in a predicament. She could drink her coffee black, but—she might die. She could shower, get dressed, go to the store and buy creamer, and then come home and drink coffee like a civilized person, but if she waited that long for the caffeine—she might die. She could pour the coffee into a travel mug, go to the store in her pajamas, buy creamer, go back to her car, open creamer, pour it into her coffee, and then drink it. This seemed like the best option. How many people were going to be at Marget's Grocery on a Tuesday morning?

Everyone. Thank God she had had the presence of mind to brush her teeth and put on a bra, but she was still in pajamas and flip-flops when she encountered everyone she'd ever known on the island—everyone who wasn't out fishing that is.

Most of them were standing around in huddles, and most of them were drinking coffee. Her mouth salivated as she hustled to the dairy section. *I should really quit coffee,* she thought. *I am too dependent.* Then she laughed at herself. *Don't be ridiculous. I'm a teacher. Without coffee—I would die.*

She was on her way to the long line at the checkout, creamer in hand, when she noticed two things. One, the whoopie pies were on sale. Two, the gaggle of men surrounding the whoopie pies were talking about Kevin Linville. She stopped. For both reasons. For several seconds, she was able to just stand there listening. They were too caught up in their drama to notice her eavesdropping, and she clearly heard, "PeeWee's all in a panic, says he thinks he might be dead," and then, "Nah, the guy ain't dead, he just turned tail and run," and then, "Came to his senses then." The last speaker looked up abruptly, finally noticing Emily standing there with her creamer.

"Excuse me," she said awkwardly, reaching between them, "just trying to get to the whoopie pies." She usually liked to pick over the whoopie pies, get the one with the most creme filling, but under the circumstances, she just grabbed the first one she touched. The men stayed silent until she was at least fifteen feet away. She heard their murmur pick back up, but couldn't make out what they were saying.

As she waited in the checkout line, she strained to hear other conversations going on around her, but could only get bits and pieces, and even these she wondered if she was just guessing at what she heard. Was "turned tail for Nautikus" really "darn sale on asparagus"? She thought she heard "Harley dumped him," which could have been "gnarly pumpkin"? Was her brain working too hard to make all of her observations fit with the narrative her brain was forming? She was glad she wasn't a detective. Aurora Teagarden made it seem so easy. As she thought about Aurora, she thought about the woman Hallmark had cast to play her, and how *wrong* they had gotten it, how the Hallmark Aurora didn't look anything like the *real* Aurora, and this line of thinking put a grimace on her face, one that alarmed Marget, who was running the register.

"Don't worry, dear. He'll turn up."

Emily startled out of her reverie. Marget was holding her hand out. At first, Emily thought she meant to shake, but then she realized Marget just wanted to scan the whoopie pie Emily was clutching possessively. Emily handed her treat over to the proprietor. "I'm sorry, what?"

"Oh, you just looked so worried, dear. I figured you'd just heard the news, and I was saying, people wander off all the time, especially people who *aren't from here.*" She put a knowing inflection on her last three words. "He'll turn up. Don't worry."

This is my chance. What would Aurora ask? Emily tried to act nonchalantly as she slid her card through the slot—no chip readers on the island, not yet. "How do we know he's missing?"

"I don't know that he is, but Harley hasn't seen him since yesterday, so she's all in a tizzy." She leaned across the counter conspiratorially as she handed Emily her receipt. "You know how those Hopkins can be."

Emily forced a smile, nodded, and then walked away. Even if she'd been able to think of another question, which she probably would've been able to if she'd had her coffee already, she couldn't stand there holding up the line.

She knew what she had to do. Hustle back to her car. Pour her dollop of dairy into her cup of joe, and then go see Kim. Kim would know.

It turned out that one dollop wasn't enough. But three did the trick, and soon Emily was feeling *much* better.

The Pizza Place wasn't open yet, of course, but Emily scaled the outside steps to Kim's outside door. She knocked on it, wondering if she was crossing some sort of island etiquette line. Judging by the look on Kim's face, she wasn't.

"Hiya! Wasn't expecting you! Come on in!" Kim sounded positively thrilled to see her. Emily settled onto a stool at her kitchen island.

"Want some coffee?" Kim asked.

"Do you have creamer?"

Kim shared an idiom about a bear defecating in the woods, and then a hand flew up to her mouth. "Sorry, I try not to swear in front of you."

Emily smiled. "It's OK. You're not offending me."

Kim set three flavored coffee creamers in front of Emily, along with a steaming cup of coffee.

Oh, today is turning out to be such *a good day.* "So, I'm really not here for a social call. I was wondering what you know about Kevin Linville."

Kim looked up quickly. "Why, what happened?"

For the first time, Emily knew something about island happenings before an islander. Maybe she was truly *becoming* an islander. "I'm not sure. I was just at Marget's, and people were talking, and it sounds like he's missing."

"Missing? Really?" She looked thoughtful, pensive even.

"Apparently, his girlfriend, Harley, hasn't seen him since yesterday."

"Huh."

"What? What do you know?"

Kim looked at her. "I don't *know* anything, but Caleb said he heard a gunshot yesterday morning, out on the water."

"A *gunshot*?" Emily couldn't believe it. Suddenly this wasn't fun anymore. She felt sick to her stomach. "Is he sure?"

Kim shrugged. "Pretty sure. The kid's no dummy."

"No, I know that. I didn't mean to suggest he was, I just … a *gunshot*? As in, someone *shot* at something on the water?"

Kim took a sip of her coffee. "Oh, I wouldn't worry about it. No one would actually *shoot* Kevin, or anyone else for that matter. I'm just thinking maybe someone shot a gun to scare him. And maybe he just left?"

Emily thought for a second. "Are the cops involved?"

Kim snickered. "What cops?"

Emily knew she was making a dig at the island's only cop, a sheriff who preferred to take a hands-off approach to law enforcement.

"The State Police?"

Kim scrunched up her face. "Don't be silly. No need to involve the police. The guy probably just decided Harley wasn't worth it and went to fish somewhere else."

Emily didn't say anything, and Kim gave her a grave look. "Emily, do *not* call the cops. Don't get involved in this *at all*."

Emily had no intention of calling the cops or of getting involved, but she couldn't help thinking that in some ways, the waters around Piercehaven, if not the island itself, sometimes resembled the Wild West.

TRESPASS

"Now, let's talk about your hosting chart," Kim said, getting back to wedding business. "Your aunt Melinda is allergic to dogs, right ..."

Chapter 21

Emily was so excited to see James that she got to his house before he even got home. She thought this might annoy him, to get home and find her sitting in her car waiting for him, so she drove around the nearby streets, waiting for his truck to appear. She drove past PeeWee's house, feeling like quite the snoop, but there was nothing to see. The place was buttoned up tight, no people in sight.

When James's truck did appear, she thought of her cat Daisy and how she would wait patiently at the end of the couch for a mouse to reappear so she could pounce. She drove around a few more minutes, to give him time to settle in. She wanted to pounce on him, but she didn't want him to feel like a trapped mouse.

Finally, she gave in and pulled into his driveway.

"Come in!" he hollered before she'd even knocked.

She found him in the kitchen.

"Why were you driving around the neighborhood?" he asked while flipping through his mail.

Well, that's *embarrassing.* When in doubt, just tell the truth. "I was just early, and didn't want to annoy you, so I drove around a little."

He gave her a quick smile, and then crossed the room and kissed her. "You wouldn't have annoyed me. Don't be silly. Soon you'll be living here, and you'll always be here when I get home from work." He kissed her again. "And I can't wait." He stepped back, looking at her with his eyes full of question. "Are you OK?"

The sternman appeared in the kitchen then, significantly startling Emily.

"Don't mind me, just passing through."

"No problem, Lucas," James said.

He bent to grab a beer out of the fridge.

Emily waited till he'd gone upstairs to ask, "You let him keep beer in here?"

James rolled his eyes. "Yes. He lives here, and I'm not his mother. Now, you OK?"

"Yes and no. I'm fine, really, but I've been hearing lots of scary stuff about Kevin Linville."

A peculiar expression came over James's face then, one she hadn't seen before. It sort of froze in a forced deadpan. "What stuff?" he asked through a tight jaw.

"That he's missing. That there was a gunshot yesterday morning ..." And then, bizarrely, she remembered waking up to something the morning before. She hadn't thought of it all day, but now that she was talking to James, she was certain that the shot had been what had awoken her.

"What?" James asked. "What else?"

"That's it, I think. I don't really know anything else. I'm just worried."

James made a *pfft* sound and stepped back. "I wouldn't worry about Kevin Linville. Hopefully, he just went back to whatever rock he crawled out from under."

"Enough!" Emily said, the sharpness in her voice surprising even her. "The guy's a human being. And he's not even a lowlife. He's got his own boat, so he must be intelligent and hardworking, right—"

"Please stop," James said calmly, with no anger in his voice. "I love you, but you have no idea what you're talking about. His father bought him that boat, and I never said he was a lowlife. I said he shouldn't be in our waters—"

153

"But you're acting like, if something bad happened to him, then he deserved it, that he doesn't get a shot at the grace and mercy the rest of us get."

James leaned back on this kitchen counter and crossed his arms. "I'm not saying anything like that. He can have all the mercy and grace he wants—just as soon as he gets out of our waters."

Emily took a deep breath. *I have to stop this conversation. We are not even speaking the same language. This is going to go on forever and get us nowhere.* "OK."

"OK?" He looked doubtful.

"Yeah, OK. I don't want to argue. I know you know more about this than I do." *Support James.* She took a deep breath. "I am just worried about the guy."

James gave her a long look, which was interrupted by an overly enthusiastic banging on the door. The hair on the back of her neck stood up. James instinctively stepped between her and the door and then cautiously made his way toward it. He didn't get there before it was flung open to reveal a pale-faced PeeWee.

Emily stepped up beside James.

"What's wrong?" James asked, and, to his credit, Emily thought, sounded genuinely concerned.

PeeWee took three big-for-his-legs, angry steps toward James and then looked up at him. If the situation hadn't been so tense, it would have been funny—a middle-aged, pudgy David trying to intimidate Goliath. But the panic written all over PeeWee took away the humor.

"You know what's wrong," he practically hissed.

James pointed at the door. "Either tell me what happened or get out of my house."

PeeWee looked unsure of himself. He leaned back. "They found the boat."

"Linville's?"

PeeWee nodded. "Caught up on some rocks on the north side."

James looked thoughtful, as if he was processing something complicated. Then he said calmly, "Sorry to hear that."

PeeWee's rage returned. "No, you're not! You're not sorry about anything! You bunch of Jesus freaks"—he looked at Emily as he spat this last part—"acting all holier than thou, and you killed him! You actually killed a man, you bunch of psychos!"

Emily felt cold all of a sudden. She reached out to steady herself on the wall.

"I assure you, I haven't killed anyone."

"You fish right by me! You couldn't possibly have *not* seen something. So it was either you or Brent." He was screaming, so totally unhinged that spit flew out of his mouth as he hollered. "Was it? Was it Brent? I'll kill him! I'll kill that piece of …" A string of expletives left his mouth, reminding Emily of the missing lobsterman's piratic vocabulary.

"PeeWee," James said calmly, but firmly, "take a step back. I told you, I didn't do anything to anyone."

PeeWee leaned in even closer. Emily was certain James could smell his breath. "Maybe not, but you sure know who did." He stepped back. "This isn't over, Gagnon. I will find out who did it, and they will pay."

Emily hadn't heard Lucas come down the stairs, so he must have been sneaky about it, but there he was on the bottom landing, cracking his knuckles. "Everything OK here, Capt?"

James nodded. "Absolutely. Mr. Hopkins here was just leaving."

PeeWee looked at Lucas, looked at James, and then turned and stomped out of the house, leaving the door open.

Chapter 22

Emily spent a third of the night tossing and turning, a third in prayer, and only a third actually asleep, so when a knock on her door woke her up at eight, she wasn't pleased. She staggered down her steps, picked up Daisy so she wouldn't escape, and with bleary eyes opened the door.

Two uniformed officers, one man and one woman, stood before her. She blinked. They weren't State Police. She could tell by the uniforms.

"Good morning, ma'am," the woman said. "We're with Marine Police. I am Officer Taylor Hebert"—she pronounced her French name "a bear"—"and this is Chad LaBelle. We're from Vinalhaven," she added, as if that might endear them to Emily. "May we come in?"

Emily didn't really want them to come in and was glad one of them was a woman. She stepped back, wondering if, had they both been men, she would have had the courage to decline their offer of an indoor visit. "Have a seat," Emily said, "you mind if I put some coffee on?"

"No, go right ahead," Officer Hebert said, looking around Emily's living room. "Nice place."

"Thanks," Emily said over her shoulder from the kitchen. "It's not mine."

She put Daisy down, got the miracle juice brewing, and then grudgingly returned to the living room to see that neither of her guests had taken her up on her offer of a seat. "How can I help you?" She folded her arms self-consciously across her chest, wishing she'd put on a bra before rushing down the stairs.

"Do you know Kevin Linville?" Officer Hebert asked.

"I do not."

"Are you aware that his boat was found adrift yesterday?"

"Yes."

Hebert scribbled on her notepad. "How did you find this out?"

"Wasn't it on the news?" Emily figured it had to have been.

"Is that how you found out?"

"So it was on the news?"

Hebert nodded impatiently.

"I don't have television. PeeWee told me."

She nodded, obviously knowing who PeeWee was. "Do you have any idea why his boat was found adrift?"

Emily scoffed. "No, I don't know anything about anything around here ... except grammar."

Officer LaBelle looked at her, his brow furrowed.

"I'm the island's high school English teacher," Emily explained, and then wished she hadn't. Why was she so nervous?

"Ah," he said, and went back to examining the books on her bookshelf.

"Has James Gagnon said anything to you about the boat?" Hebert asked.

Emily's chest tightened, defensive. "No. He found out about it the same time I did."

Hebert nodded, looking suspicious, as though she was fully aware of how defensive Emily had just become. "And did he say anything about hearing or seeing anything unusual on Monday morning?"

See, James? This is why you should tell me things! "Not that I remember."

Hebert couldn't have looked more skeptical, and Emily couldn't have felt more protective of James. She suddenly wanted to claw this woman's eyes out.

"He didn't mention hearing a gunshot?"

"He did not."

"And did *you* hear a gunshot?"

"Me?"

"Yeah." Hebert put her hands on her hips and looked around Emily's house. "You're pretty close to the water here, on the east side, where James and Kevin fish."

Before she could stop herself, Emily said, "*Kevin* doesn't *fish* on the east side. He's been there a few days. He's an interloper." She realized how she sounded and stopped. "What I mean is, that's PeeWee's area. Kevin's just been visiting."

"Ah-ha," Hebert said smugly, as if she were figuring things out—things that didn't even really exist to *be* figured out, because Emily and James had nothing to do with this.

Suddenly, Emily *really* didn't like Kevin Linville. She wished she'd never even heard the name. "I'm sorry that this guy's missing. I am. But I can promise you, James had nothing to do with it. And I certainly didn't. I don't know anything."

Hebert paused, staring at Emily, with a smirk on her face.

Is she trying to intimidate me?

"OK then." Hebert pulled a card out of her pocket. "If you hear anything, give us a call?"

Emily took the card, but didn't agree to anything.

Hebert turned toward the door, where LaBelle was already waiting with his hand on the knob. He couldn't have looked less suspicious of Emily. In fact, he looked bored with the whole ordeal. Emily wondered if maybe he, being from Vinalhaven, was on the lobstermen's side here. And with that thought, she realized that on some level, she knew that something had happened to Kevin Linville, and she knew that some lobsterman had made it happen.

"Wait."

Hebert turned around, an eyebrow raised.

"Has anyone checked Nautikus?"

Hebert jerked her head back as if dodging a punch. "Yes, ma'am, we know how to do our job."

"And he's not there?"

Hebert rolled her eyes. "No. No one has seen him."

"But … did you actually go *look* for him there?"

Hebert took a step backward. "We'll do our job, Miss Morse. You do yours."

LaBelle gave Emily a polite nod and then opened the door for his partner. Daisy shot out through the opening like a bullet.

TRESPASS

It was the longest day of her life. The first few hours of it were spent trying to find Daisy. Emily was miserable, angry, and impatient as she trudged through the tall grass and continuously stubbed her toes on rocks, looking for her female tabby.

When she finally found the cat, she was incredibly relieved and incredibly glad that the search was over and she could get on with her day. But once she was back inside, she wished she hadn't found the cat so quickly. Because *now* what was she going to do? She couldn't do *anything* except wonder about Kevin Linville.

Not a single cell in her body believed that James had something to do with his disappearance, but did he know more than he was saying? Of course he did.

She got a pad of paper and a pen and sat down.

She wrote at the top, "Did someone shoot Kevin Linville?"

Then she stared at the rest of the blank page. What was she doing? She wasn't a detective, and she had no desire to be one. But, what else was she going to do until James got home? Worry? Analyze a situation she didn't know enough about to analyze? If she was going to do that, she might as well do it in an orderly fashion.

She wrote on the page, "Did James hear gunshot?"

Yes. He most definitely had. Because he was on the water, and gunshots are loud. If she heard it from her bedroom, he definitely heard it from his boat. *See? I'm making progress.*

She tore the sheet off, crumpled it, and threw it on the floor, an action that was oddly satisfying. She wondered if that was how the poets did it.

On the new sheet, she wrote, "Did someone shoot Kevin Linville?" and then underneath that, "James, and a bunch of other people, heard gunshot at approximately 6:30 a.m." She wasn't sure that's when the gun had fired, but that's when she'd woken up.

She chewed on her pen.

She wrote, "Did James see anything?"

She had no idea. He could've been looking the other way. He could've been too far away to see anything. And if he'd heard the gunshot and then looked, it might have been too late to see anything. *But,* if he'd heard a gunshot and then seen a man fall in the water, he would have tried to help the man, no matter what man it was. And if he'd heard a gunshot, and then seen an empty boat, he would've tried to help the man who'd been on it. She was sure of it. Wasn't she? He wouldn't have just sailed away from such a crisis. Right? No, he wouldn't have.

So, she wrote, "No, he didn't see anything."

James had heard the gunshot, but he hadn't seen anything. So why was he acting so suspiciously? Because he knew something. He knew something he hadn't seen or heard for himself. Maybe he just had a theory. Maybe he just had suspicions. That would be enough to drive him crazy, wouldn't it?

At the bottom of the page, she wrote, "Support James." Then she ripped this page off the pad, crumpled it, and threw it on the floor beside the first fallen soldier. She sighed, leaned back on her couch, and began the long wait for James to come ashore.

Chapter 23

She got to James's house at a quarter past four, and there were two trucks in the driveway: his and his sternman's. Emily groaned. Why was the sternman always around when she decided to cook? She hefted the slow cooker out of her passenger side seat and carried her beef stew to the door. Not exactly July food, but it was one of James's favorites.

Lucas opened the door for her. "All right!" he called out. "She brought food!" He took the Crock-Pot from her hands and headed for the kitchen.

Emily caught a glimpse of James over Lucas's shoulder and gave him a crooked smile. He met her in the hallway and gave her a hug and a kiss that she sorely needed. He let go of her, and she followed him into the kitchen to see that Lucas was already spooning some of her stew into a bowl. But he'd only gotten out one bowl and one spoon.

TRESPASS

James reached into his cupboard and pulled out two new bowls, and handed her one. She wasn't hungry, had been munching all day, but she took it anyway. "Thanks."

"You OK?"

"Yeah. So I had a visit from the Marine Police today."

James groaned. He filled a bowl with stew and then handed it to Emily, and took her empty bowl from her hands. She sat and looked down at the food. Mushy potatoes had never looked less appetizing.

"Got some kick to it!" Lucas exclaimed through a full mouth. He got up to get a beer.

James sat down beside her. "I'm sorry that happened."

Emily thought he might be reluctant to have this conversation in front of his sternman, but she saw no signs of this being true.

"They came to see us on the water too."

"They did? What did you say?"

James looked, of all things, amused. "I said nothing. I don't know anything *to* say. I answered their questions, but I wasn't much help."

"Stupid Marine Po-Po," Lucas said.

"What did they ask you?"

"Lobster wardens!" Lucas exclaimed, but it sounded like "lob-stah wah-dahns."

"They asked if I knew Linville, if I'd seen him that morning, if I'd heard the shot, if I knew where he was …"

"And?"

"And what?"

"And what did you say?"

James swallowed his bite. "I told you. I told them the truth."

"That you didn't really know Kevin, that you hadn't seen him that morning, that you did hear the shot, and that you don't know where he is?"

James gave her a long look. "Yeah. Pretty much. How did you know I heard the shot?"

"*Everyone* heard the shot, man," Lucas said.

"How do you know?" Emily cried. "You weren't even there!"

Lucas looked at her over the top of the bowl he was now drinking out of. He swallowed. "I know things."

"Did the lobster wardens question you too?" she asked.

He beamed, obviously proud that she'd used his phrase, even though she'd pronounced it without six inches of Downeast accent piled on top. "Course," he said. (*Cawss.*)

"Well, you took that day off. Does that make them suspicious?"

167

Lucas laughed so loudly that Emily had to resist the urge to cover her ears. She didn't understand why that was so funny.

"The police know that he's just a sternman," James said softly.

Well, that sounds a little patronizing.

Lucas didn't look offended.

"Why does that matter?" Emily asked.

James put his spoon down and looked at her. "Because no sternman from the mainland is going to care enough about a territory dispute to get involved."

"Territory dispute?" she repeated. "Sounds like the range wars of the old west."

James shrugged. "Not that different, I suppose."

"So you did hear the shot?"

James nodded.

Emily stood up, pushing her chair back from her untouched stew. "Let's go for a walk."

James smirked knowingly and stood to join her. "Save some for me," he said to Lucas.

"Of course," Lucas said, and helped himself to more.

James followed her out the door. "Well, at least I'm walking more now that I'm hosting a sternman."

Emily ignored this comment and turned to face him before they'd even gotten to the end of the driveway. "James, I am *begging* you. Please tell me what you know. I felt so awkward today when they came to question me. I was actually scared. I felt like I should lie to cover for you—"

He took her hands in his. "I would *never* ask you to lie."

"I know that." She felt tears coming and staved them off. "But I *would*. God help me, I *would*. And I don't know the truth. I mean, of course, I know that you didn't hurt anyone, but I don't really know what happened, so when they questioned me, I just didn't know what to say."

He wrapped his arms around her then and pulled her head to his chest. It felt so good to rest it there, and she didn't want to move.

"Are we going to walk, or just stand in my driveway?"

She giggled and pulled herself up.

He took her hand and led her to the street. "You know I love you, right?"

She wasn't always confident of this, but she knew what she was supposed to say. "Sure."

"And do you trust me?"

Again, she wanted to say, "Mostly," but that would have been the wrong answer. "Yes."

"Then just let me deal with this. Try not to worry about it. I promise you, we will not be affected by this."

"But we're already affected—"

He stopped walking, turned to her, and gently put a finger to her lips. Then he kissed her. "Please," he said softly, "let it go."

Chapter 24

Emily had a wedding planning meeting with Kim scheduled for Friday morning. She couldn't wait. *Anything* to get her mind off this Linville mess. Though no one seemed to be talking about it anymore, and though the Marine Police had vanished just as quickly as they'd appeared, *Emily* could think about nothing else. Had a man really been killed? And were people really just going to let that go? She didn't know if she wanted to live in a place that worked that way. She didn't know if she *could* live in a place that worked that way. And she knew that James wouldn't live anywhere else, and even if he could, she couldn't ask him to. It was eating her up inside.

So talking about wedding stuff was just the distraction she needed.

But all Kim wanted to talk about was Kevin Linville.

TRESPASS

Kim had her put on the dress and the shoes. Of course, The Pizza Place hadn't yet opened for the day, but it still felt incredibly bizarre changing in its dining room. Emily reached around and zipped up the back of her dress as far as she could. "Can you zip me up the rest of the way?"

"Don't need to. I'm just checking the length. Oh yeah, this has definitely got to come up a bit. Hang on." She lay on the floor and started pinning. Her mouth full of pins, she said, "James must have told you *something*."

Emily groaned. She was embarrassed that he hadn't told her anything. "No, really. I know less than nothing."

Kim patted Emily's calf. Emily didn't think her calf had ever been patted before.

"Well, you can't blame him for trying to keep you out of it. He's just trying to protect you."

"Protect me from what?" Emily didn't know what she meant. Protect her from drama? From scandal? Or from some sort of crime that might come with knowing too much?

"Oh, just from all the gossips. If people thought you knew something, they'd never leave you alone."

"Really? 'Cause it seems people are being pretty tight-lipped about it."

"Those *close* to the situation are tight-lipped. That's normal, especially for the men, but the rest of us want to know the scoop." She tittered. "So be grateful you have no beans to spill."

"Yeah, grateful."

"You know people are saying that your church split because of Linville?"

"What?" Emily cried indignantly. "First of all, our church didn't *split*. We *multiplied*."

Kim didn't say anything, but her hands were quite busy.

Emily looked down at her, but couldn't see her head. "And second, why would we divide over that? That doesn't even make sense."

"I don't know," Kim said. "Two big things happen on the island, and people assume they must be related."

"Half of us moving out of Abe's basement is a big thing?"

Kim pulled her head out from under the dress. Her eyebrows were raised. "You know Piercehaven. Not much happens around he-ah."

Emily laughed and then felt guilty for it.

"What's wrong?" Kim asked.

"I just feel guilty being happy when a man is missing."

"Missing?" Kim said. "Pretty sure he's dead."

Emily was shocked. Of course, the idea had occurred to her a zillion times, but she was still surprised to hear Kim say it. "Do you really think so?"

Kim shrugged and stood up. "You can get dressed now. I don't see any other scenario that has him leaving his boat adrift."

Emily thought for a minute. "Do you know anyone on Nautikus?"

Kim curled her lip as if Emily had asked her if she was related to anyone in Nineveh. "No. Why?"

"Because I'm wondering if he just went home. I mean, isn't that what people wanted?"

"Again, he wouldn't go home and just leave the boat. Now, Abe says he'll have the rehearsal dinner in his basement, if you want, and that his family will take care of clean up and set up. So we just need some people to bring a few extra dishes for those from your family who won't want to bring food."

Emily nodded, thinking that it was so silly to be discussing potlucks if a man had been murdered.

Kim, apparently reading her mind, said, "Didn't the police check Nautikus?"

"They said they did. But it sounded as though they just asked people there if anyone had seen him. I don't think they actually went there to look for him. At least, they hadn't when I talked to them."

"Makes sense."

"What makes sense?"

"That they don't want to go to Nautikus. Nobody wants to go to Nautikus. But let's talk about something good." She sucked in a bunch of air. "So, Greg and I are going to try to make things work."

"Really? Why didn't you say so a long time ago? That's wonderful!"

"Yeah, it is. I think. Maybe." She giggled. "Me and Caleb are moving back in. We've already started, so next time you want to come over for coffee in your pajamas, come there."

"I don't even know where *there* is."

Kim sat down at the nearest table and drew her a map, showing her a clear route from The Pizza Place to her old/new house. Then Kim made a rehearsal dinner potluck chart, assigning dishes to such fortunate souls as Chloe's mother and Brent's wife. Emily wondered just how much luck was involved if people were assigned specific dishes. Wasn't it then more of a "pot-duty"? Then she decided this sounded like a phrase one might use when toilet training a toddler, and giggled.

She pulled on her flannel shirt and sat opposite Kim.

"You all right?" Kim asked, one eyebrow perked.

"Honestly?" Emily felt a bit of hysterical laughter coming on. She couldn't stop smiling, even though she felt anything but smiley on the inside. "I'm not sure I'm all right at all. I'm freaking out. Do I really want to marry a man who won't tell me things? A man who might be helping to cover up a murder? Do I really want to live on an island that thinks it's perfectly OK to ignore a *murder* because someone stole someone's stupid lobsters? Or an island that thinks my basement church split over lobster territories?" Her voice was high-pitched, she felt herself slipping out of control, and then the tears came.

Kim smiled sympathetically. "I think this is just pre-wedding jitters."

Emily shrieked out a laugh. "Pre-wedding jitters? Oh, really? So every bride worries about whether or not her husband witnessed a murder and whether or not she's going to spend the rest of her life, raise her kids even, trapped on an island with a bunch of psychopaths?"

Kim leaned back.

Emily gasped for air. "Sorry. I didn't mean that. I'm just … like I said … losing it a little."

Kim closed her notebook and put her papers in a pile. "Maybe we should finish this later."

"Kim, I'm sorry," she tried.

Kim stood. "It's OK, really. We'll finish when you're feeling better." And without looking at her, Kim walked away.

Great job, she thought to herself as she wiped at her eyes with the backs of her hands. *Your first grownup friend on the island, and you just called her a psychopath.*

She sat there for several minutes, and then decided she couldn't walk away and leave things like this. She gingerly approached the open kitchen doorway.

At first, she couldn't see anyone, but then she saw a man who must have been Kim's father. He nodded at her, and then hollered, "Kimmy!" over his shoulder.

Kim approached. "I thought you'd left."

Emily took a shaky breath. "I know. Maybe I should've. I just couldn't leave like that. I'm really sorry I said what I said. I didn't mean it. I obviously don't think you're a psychopath. I wouldn't let a psychopath plan my wedding."

Kim laughed. "You were so desperate, you would have let Frankenstein plan your wedding, but I get it."

"So can you forgive me?"

TRESPASS

Kim wiped her hands on her apron even though they looked clean and dry. "Yeah, of course. I think I was so upset because, well, because you're right."

Emily blinked. About which part?

"I just never really thought about it before. If something bad did happen to that guy, then you're right that we shouldn't just say he got what he deserved. *If* something happened to him, he didn't deserve that." She looked Emily in the eye for the first time since Emily had first said the word psychopath. "But you're wrong about James. He's a good man. If you let him get away because of this, you'll regret it forever."

Chapter 25

Emily was a ball of nerves on Sunday morning. Absurdly, her biggest fear was that no one was going to show up. That it would just be her and James, singing hymns in the living room.

Though it wasn't her house yet, she almost felt as though it was, and she got there early to make coffee. She asked James if he had a big platter to arrange the donuts on, and he laughed at her. She thought about putting them in a bowl, but then realized that was ridiculous. So she just left them in their boxes. There would be no pretense around here. Those stale donuts came from Marget's, and in their boxes they would stay until some undiscerning donut consumer changed that.

Her instinct was to straighten up, but there was nothing crooked in sight. James kept his house neat as a pin. He was unfolding metal chairs in his living room when the sternman came downstairs.

"When's this shindig going to start?" Lucas flopped down on the couch.

Emily tried to hide her surprise.

"Any minute now," James said. Then he went into the kitchen.

Emily followed him. "Maybe you were right," she muttered.

"Probably." He grabbed a coffee mug and filled it. "About what?"

"Lucas probably wouldn't have followed us to a church building, but it appears he's going to join us here?"

"Certainly seems that way."

She refilled her own cup.

"Am I allowed to drink beer at this thing?" Lucas called out.

James headed back into the living room. "Do you really want to drink beer at ten o'clock in the morning?"

"Only if I'm not allowed to," he said with a broad grin.

"Then you are definitely allowed to." James sat down and opened his Bible, which he placed on a TV tray table in front of him.

And then the people started arriving, and there were bunches of them, a few Emily hadn't even seen before. Kim, Caleb, and Greg came first. Kim looked overwhelmed. Caleb looked as though he'd rather be anywhere else. And Greg looked as though he didn't feel well. Emily looked at him carefully. *He looks like he's lost weight.* His skin was more gray than red now, and she wondered if he was truly ill. James and he shared a somber handshake, which Emily thought lasted much longer than most handshakes did. Something seemed to pass between the two men, some sort of understanding. MacKenzie and her mom, Heather, were next through the door. Then the Stevensons and the Crocketts and the Greenlaws and the Browns—who lived two doors down from James, and so naturally, on their way by, had scooped up the neighbor in the middle. James ran down his basement stairs to fetch more chairs. And then the highpoint of Emily's day—Chloe's family arrived with Thomas in tow. Emily shrieked with delight, gave him a bear hug, and welcomed him profusely. Chloe beamed with pride that she'd actually gotten him there. Thomas and Caleb had a bit of a stare down, which ended the minute Chloe sat down beside Thomas, as if Caleb wasn't even in the room.

Emily offered everyone coffee and donuts, and the donuts disappeared faster than free lottery tickets. When James called the meeting to order, Emily was in the kitchen making the third pot of coffee. She had a moment of empathy for pastors' wives everywhere. Then she had a moment of gratitude that James wasn't really a pastor.

When she returned to the living room, Sandra Brown was unpacking a guitar. Emily hadn't even known she played, but soon she was leading them in "10,000 Reasons," and as Emily joined her neighbors in song, she felt each of her anxieties let go. The wedding? *No big deal.* The family coming? So what if they liked the island? *They don't have to like it. They don't have to live here.* And Kevin Linville? *God is still in control.* All the tightness in her chest and in her brain melted away as she sang a new song to God.

After the music, James asked if there were any prayer requests, and there were many. Three people with cancer, including one little boy. Two wayward children—they weren't really children anymore, but they were to their parents. The Browns' eight-year-old asked for prayer for his sick dog. Emily couldn't believe no one was mentioning the giant elephant on the island. So she did. "Can we pray for Kevin Linville?"

James exchanged a look with Gunner, a look Emily didn't like, a look that said they knew something she didn't. "Sure," James said, in a tone not so different from the one he'd used to promise prayer for the dog.

"Just that, wherever he is, that he is OK, and that God's will is done in that situation," Emily said.

"Sure," James said again without looking at her. "Let's all pray, then." He led them in an eloquent prayer that felt neither rushed nor drawn out. He included the dog right up front, "Father, we know you care about all your creatures, and we ask you to lay your healing hands on Max, that he would have many more good, healthy, happy years with his family."

Then, as he was winding down, he said, "And we ask you to be in this situation with Linville." He paused. "I don't know whether or not he's alive, but we pray that he is. And that you would have your hand in this situation. In Jesus' name we pray, amen."

James's head snapped up. He seemed to be in a hurry to move on. "Now, I've prepared a message today, but I don't need to do that every week. If one of you wants to share something sometime, just let me know. In the meantime, are there any topics you guys would like to explore?" He clicked his pen and looked at his living room expectantly. At first, they were reluctant to make requests, but once one did, the dam broke. Someone wanted to learn about angels. Someone else about holiness. Someone else about judging others. Jane Crockett said, "I'd like to know what the Bible says about flat earth." Lucas said, "I'd like to know more about fornication," and half the room laughed while half stayed uncomfortably silent.

After the service, Emily cornered Thomas before he could get away. "So, what did you think?"

Thomas smiled. "Not as bad as I thought it would be. Not as boring as my grandmother's church. Your sternman's a piece of work."

"He's not *my* sternman, but thanks."

"So, what do you know about Linville? Is he really dead?"

"Is that why you came? To see what I know about Kevin Linville?"

Thomas gave her his exasperated expression, a look she had missed dearly in the last month. "No, I came because Chloe *made* me. But really, what do you know?"

"Honestly, Thomas, I don't know anything. And aren't you usually the one giving me the information?"

"Yeah, but this time you're the one marrying the eyewitness."

Emily fell silent.

Thomas's smile faded, as if he realized he'd said too much. "So they say," he added.

"Yeah, sorry," Emily said, trying to keep the conversation light when she felt anything but. "I really don't know anything."

Thomas looked as though he felt awful. "I'm sorry, Miss M. I shouldn't have opened my big mouth. I don't know if he really saw anything. He just fishes close to Peewee's area, and Linville was obviously *in* PeeWee's area, so ... it's all just talk, I'm sure."

Chloe approached then, and Emily silently thanked God for the interruption.

"Whatchu guys talking about?"

Emily forced her teacher smile. "Oh, Thomas here was just promising me that he's going to come to church every week."

Chloe lit up. "Nuh-uh!"

Thomas smiled. "We'll see."

Chapter 26

By Tuesday, there was still no word of Kevin Linville's whereabouts. And no one seemed to be particularly concerned about them either. Emily wondered how Harley Hopkins was doing, even though she didn't know her.

She was thinking about Harley when she ran into Juniper and Jake at the grocery store. "Hey, guys!" she said with genuine excitement. "Haven't seen you in weeks! How are you?"

"So, so good, Coach!"

Emily loved that Juniper still called her coach, even though Emily might never get to coach her again. In September, the windmills would be operational, and the Jasper family would move off the island just as easily as they had come.

"I just got back from pitching camp in Pennsylvania, and it was *so, so* good. I've gained so much speed, and I have a knuckleball now!"

"Wow! Congratulations!"

"And she's *almost* got a screwball," proud Dad said.

"*Dad*," Juniper scolded, but her smile suggested she enjoyed the praise even as her rosy cheeks said it embarrassed her. "Yeah, *almost*. Flies right at the batter and scares the snot out of them. Trouble is, sometimes I hit the batter." She giggled. "But I'm still working on that."

"We've got some news for you too," Jake said.

"Oh?"

"Yeah, Juniper and I have talked about it a lot." He looked down at his daughter. "She's thought about it a lot, and she's decided she wants to graduate from Piercehaven."

"What?" Emily felt her eyes grow wide. "Really?" Her heart leapt at the thought. She stepped forward and embraced Juniper, who hugged her back. Emily stepped back and looked at her. "Are you sure? This is a huge decision!"

"I'm sure," Juniper said. "I think we can take states this year."

Emily wasn't so sure about this, but her smile didn't fade any.

"She might get the start at Mattawooptock this year, or she might not. But she's pretty confident she'll get to pitch here in

Piercehaven, and like she said, a state championship is a state championship, no matter what size the school, and we both think we've got a shot next year. Richmond isn't unbeatable."

She thought that indeed, Richmond was entirely unbeatable, but she wasn't going to argue. "Juniper, that just makes me so, so happy. But you continue to give it some thought, and whatever you decide is best for you, I'll support, OK?"

"OK, Coach."

Emily started to push her cart away, but Jake was still talking. "Just so you know, she's playing with Mattawooptock in a few weekend tournaments this summer, so don't spread the good news around, or they'll bench her." He laughed.

It was so good to talk to someone she knew wasn't thinking about Kevin Linville. They probably didn't even know anything about him. How refreshing.

"So awesome. Let me know when the games are. I would love to come watch."

They exchanged parting pleasantries, and Emily wheeled her cart into the next aisle, where she almost smacked into Sydney and Harley Hopkins, and the joyous Juniper Jasper smile fell off her face. "Hi, ladies," she said softly.

"Hi, Coach," Sydney said.

"You must be Harley," Emily said, holding out her hand. "I'm Emily Morse, Syd's English teacher and softball coach."

Harley shook her hand. "Nice to meet you."

Emily looked at her closely. She looked like a slightly older, slightly rounder, red-headed version of Sydney. But what stood out to Emily was just how not-sad she seemed. "How are you ladies doing?" she asked, because she wanted to keep the conversation going.

"Bored," Sydney said quickly, and Harley elbowed her.

"Fine," Harley said.

"Harley, I wanted to say how sorry I was to hear about Kevin. I'm praying they find him soon."

She looked at the floor and tucked her long hair behind her ear. "Thanks."

"You must be worried sick."

Harley didn't look up. "Yeah."

Sydney was staring at her sister.

Emily couldn't put her finger on it, but something was off. Sydney didn't behave like most girls on a good day, and this was probably not a good day, but still—they were just acting oddly, somehow *too light* for the circumstances. Worrying about Kevin Linville was keeping Emily up nights. But here was Harley Hopkins, looking well-rested, with matching clothes and flawless makeup. *Of course, maybe the girl's just a sociopath. Maybe she's the one who shot him.*

"We should get going," Harley said.

"Yeah, we should get going," Sydney repeated.

"OK, well you ladies take care. Nice to meet you, Harley."

They scurried past her.

"Yeah, see you at basketball, Miss M!"

"Hey, girls?" Emily turned around.

So did they, obviously against their wishes.

"I was just wondering, has anyone checked Nautikus?"

"What?" Harley said.

"I was thinking. Maybe he got scared and just went home. Didn't know if you'd checked there."

"Um, I think I would know if he just went home," Harley said with a sarcastic tone Emily knew well from Sydney. She wondered who had taught the tone to whom, or if they'd both just been born with it.

"Yeah, that's what I figured," Emily said with intentional ambiguity. "You would know, wouldn't you?"

Chapter 27

After another almost sleepless night, Emily had made up her mind: she was going to Nautikus. She didn't understand why no one else was doing it, and she had to know for herself. And she couldn't ask the sheriff or Marine Patrol to do it, because it would be akin to "telling them how to do their jobs." Plus, she didn't really want to deal with the sheriff—ever again. He'd proven to be less than helpful back when she'd needed his help more than she needed it now. And she really didn't want to call Marine Patrol stupid. They probably *did* have a reason for not going to check Nautikus. She just didn't know what it was.

She went to the library to look up the Nautikus ferry schedule. (She couldn't do it at her house because she had no Wi-Fi.) The Nautikus ferry also departed from the Camden terminal, but she was dismayed to see that the Nautikus ferry only ran once a month. *Once a month?* How was that even possible? So no one ever went there? Or left there? *Unless they have their own boats. Like Kevin did. But Kevin left his here.* Maybe he wasn't there. How would he surreptitiously get there? She read the fine print and saw that the ferry stayed docked on Nautikus for anywhere from forty-five minutes to two hours. So, in theory, she could ride the ferry there, spend forty-five minutes snooping around, and then hop the ferry back. Unless she missed the ferry. Then she'd need to call for help, and there would be no denying why she'd gone there. That was probably a moot point, though, as the next ferry didn't run for two weeks. No way she was going to wait that long.

She had another thought and searched for private water taxis to Nautikus. Sure enough, there was one, but a round trip cost two hundred dollars. At first, she thought she was obviously in the wrong line of work, but then she thought, *Probably not many people making that trip.*

So maybe she *wasn't* going to Nautikus.

But she had to.

At dinner, eating ravioli with James and Lucas, she wondered how to broach the subject. She decided to go in sideways. "Why was Kevin so stubborn?"

James closed his eyes, obviously exasperated. "Are we *ever* going to stop talking about him?"

"Yes, the second they find him alive and well. Now, why was he so stubborn? Why didn't he just go fish somewhere else? Are Piercehaven lobsters somehow better than other Maine lobsters?"

James smirked. "Piercehaven lobsters are *definitely* better than other lobsters, but that's not why he stayed." He took a deep breath. "He stayed because PeeWee wouldn't let Harley move to Nautikus, and because PeeWee blew a bunch of smoke up Kevin's butt, saying that because PeeWee had a right to fish there, so did Kevin."

Lucas was laughing.

"What?" James said.

"Smoke up his butt. You guys will go out of your way not to swear."

James closed his eyes, looking for a second like a tired middle school teacher. Then he opened them again. "Anyway, I think PeeWee, scared of losing his daughter to another island, convinced the guy to come fish here. Probably should have thought to have him at least paint over the giant Nautikus on his stern, but anyway. Then Harley went out with him the first few days to try to bridge the gap.

But it didn't work. Because it wasn't her boat. And they're not married."

"So, if they *had been* married, none of this would have happened?"

James chewed his ravioli slowly, staring at the ceiling, contemplating her question. Then, "No, I think it probably still wouldn't have been OK. The point is, PeeWee is an idiot. He never consulted with anyone. He was arrogant about his rights to the territory and he brought in an obnoxious outsider, I think, in part, because he knew his girls were never going to fish, and he has no sons, so I think he wanted to hand his territory down to *someone*—anyone, even Kevin Linville."

"That's fascinating," Emily said and meant it. "I didn't realize there was that much to it. So"—she pushed her plate away—"I need to go to Nautikus."

Lucas guffawed. "Man, she just doesn't quit, bro," he said, his mouth full.

James looked bemused. "No, she sure doesn't. And no, you don't need to go to Nautikus."

She ignored this. "I looked at their ferry schedule …"

Both men laughed at this.

"And I don't want to wait two weeks to go. So, will you take me?"

"Who, me?" James asked.

Emily found this hysterical. Whom did he think she was asking? She looked at the perpetually-ravenous sternman. "Lucas, will you take me to Nautikus?"

Lucas, not knowing she was kidding, looked at his boss in a panic.

James put his fork down. "No one needs to go to Nautikus."

Some words came out of her then, and she wasn't quite sure where they came from. They were not premeditated, but they were quite astute, and she was proud of them. "James, do you know for sure that he's dead? Because that's the only possible reason for you to refuse to take me to Nautikus."

James blinked, surprised.

Lucas whistled. "She got you there, man."

James gave him a look that told him in no uncertain terms to stop talking.

"I do not know for certain that he is dead."

"Then take me to the island. For the life of me, I can't imagine why no one else cares enough to check."

"I'm sure Harley has checked."

"Yeah, I think she has too. And I think she knows that he's there—alive and well."

"What?" James cried.

TRESPASS

She'd never seen him so surprised. "Just my theory."

"Just your theory," he repeated. "And you're not just saying this just to get me to take you out there?"

"No. Take me, or I'm stealing your boat."

Lucas laughed. "Just take her, man."

James gave him another scalding look. "You realize that Nautikus isn't a very welcoming place?"

"You mean unlike Piercehaven?" Emily said, her tongue in her cheek.

James grew visibly defensive. "Nautikus is *nothing* like Piercehaven. People think all these islands are the same. But they're not. They're like their own little countries, with their own beliefs, their own systems, their own way of doing things."

Don't I know it.

"Nautikus doesn't welcome outsiders. There are no tourists there. We're going to stand out. Make people suspicious."

"James, I am *begging* you. I can't sleep at night. I don't want to keep praying for the man and grieving over him if he's just playing video games and eating cheese puffs on a different island."

Lucas laughed again.

James looked at him.

"Sorry, she's funny, man."

"OK," James said.

"OK?"

"Yeah, I'll take you. But I'm not giving up a fishing day. We'll go on Sunday."

"What about church?" Lucas and Emily asked in unison.

James laughed and shook his head. "Someone will cover. You want to go or not?"

Emily leapt up, ran around the table, and flung her arms around him. "Thank you, thank you!" She kissed him on the cheek and then squeezed him again.

"Easy now!" he said. "You weren't this excited when I proposed."

Chapter 28

Sunday morning, Emily leapt out of bed, looked out the window, cried out in horror, and fell back into bed. It was raining, and she could see the tops of the trees moving in the wind. No way James was going to head into deep waters today. She staggered downstairs, started the coffee, and called him anyway.

"I was going to call, but didn't want to wake you up," he said. "I guess you've figured out the bad news."

"Yeah."

"I'm sorry, honey. I'll take you next Sunday."

She fell into her wooden kitchen chair. "But next Sunday is a whole week away."

"Yeah, that's usually how Sundays work. See you soon. Get extra donuts this time. We ran out of them early last week."

"But, James," she whined, "we *get married* Saturday. Are you really going to want to go to Nautikus the day after your wedding?" And, she thought, *Am I really going to marry you before I learn the truth?*

"We don't have to go that day, if you want to wait another week."

This was hopeless. "I'll see you soon." And she hung up.

Suddenly, the wedding was all too soon. It was this giant occasion looming before her, and she wondered if she had been using the Kevin mystery, maybe just a little, to distract her from the stress of this imminent event. She shook her head. Was she really going to commit herself to this? To this man? To this island? To this way of life?

She thought about James. Yes, yes she was.

The house wasn't as packed this Sunday as it had been for their premiere, but there were some new faces. Emily was stoked to see Thomas again, and made that clear to everyone within earshot. Not very professional for an educator, but there it was. Caleb and his family returned for another visit, and Greg looked even more tired and sickly than before.

After the service, Emily talked to Kim the first chance she got.

"You excited?" Kim asked. Kim was obviously excited.

"Yes. Is Greg OK?"

"Yeah, why?"

"He just doesn't look good." Emily looked at him across the room. "Is he getting any sleep?"

Kim's smile faded. "Yeah, he's not a hundred percent right now. He says it's alcohol withdrawals ..."

"But you don't believe that?"

"Oh, I do," Kim said quickly. "I just don't know much about it. Drinking doesn't run in my family. But he's been sober for two weeks now, and it hasn't been easy. It's made him really sick."

"Has he been to the clinic? They must have something to help him with the symptoms."

"He doesn't want anything. He says that chemicals got him into this mess, so he's not going to use chemicals to get him out. Believe me, I've tried."

"Wow, well, good for him for sticking with it. Must be so hard. Your spirit is ready to be free of something, but your body is still fighting."

"It's OK. He's going to make it. *We're* going to make it. He's been so sweet to me, Emily. He's like a whole new man." She stared at him, and Emily could see the love dancing in her eyes.

"You know that part of that sweetness is Jesus, right? I mean, not that he wasn't a sweet guy before."

"Oh no, he really wasn't." She smiled wistfully. "We got together because he was hot and he had his own boat. So I liked him. Then I got pregnant, and well, that's the same island story, over and over. So I know that this new sweetness is from Jesus. It has to be. There's no other explanation. I know the man. And he's told me all about his spiritual stuff. Told me he wanted to die when we first left him, but now he feels more alive than ever. It's funny him trying to explain something to me that he doesn't even really understand. But I'm starting to believe. I mean, I guess I've always believed in God, but now I'm happy to learn more and to be a follower of Jesus. He's already had me pray with him about five times." She laughed. "Now, we just need to get Caleb on board."

"That will come. Just be patient. And keep praying. I'll keep praying too. And, Kim, congratulations. You'll never regret choosing Jesus."

TRESPASS

When all the guests had left the house—well, everyone except for the sternman—Emily collapsed on James's couch and put her feet up.

"You OK?" He picked her feet up, sat down underneath them, and then lowered them onto his lap. Then he began to rub them, which felt like heaven.

Nevertheless, she sat up and curled her feet beneath her. "We need to talk."

He looked at Lucas, and Lucas obediently scurried upstairs.

"What's up?"

"I'm not OK, James. I'm freaking out."

"About?"

She took a big breath. "I love you so much. I can't even believe how much I love you. I love you so much it hurts me, but I'm scared to marry a man who keeps secrets from me and I mean *big* secrets." She felt her voice crack and willed it steady. "I trust you, I do, but—"

"Emily, it's not my secret to keep." His face looked so tender in that moment, so vulnerable, that she knew no matter what he said next, it was going to be OK. *They* were going to be OK.

"James," she said softly, "I love you, but I just need to know that you're not covering up a murder."

He tipped his head back and closed his eyes. "I am not covering up a murder."

"Then what aren't you telling me?" She hated herself in that moment. Why couldn't she just let it go? Why couldn't she just trust him? But she had to know. "And whatever it is, I will support you."

He looked at her. "I love you too. And once I tell you, I can't *un*tell you. You will then be burdened by the knowledge just like I am."

"I would rather be burdened with knowledge than live with the anxiety of not knowing."

He nodded slowly, and then he took a big breath. "On that Monday morning, there were only three boats in the area, me, Linville, and Greg. The gunshot was loud. I know it came from nearby. I think it came from Greg. But I don't know for sure. When I looked up, both boats were moving away from me. I just figured Greg had fired a warning shot. I'm not saying that's right, but that's what I figured. I didn't know the guy might be hurt till the next day."

There it was. Now she knew. Now what was she going to do with this knowledge?

"How could the boat be motoring away from you if he'd been shot?"

James shrugged. "Easy, if the throttle was pushed forward. It's not like a gas pedal. You don't have to hold it down."

"But then wouldn't the boat have just kept going, right off into the deep sea? Until it ran out of gas? And you guys don't run out of gas often, because you don't run around on empty?"

James shook his head. "All the questions I've been asking myself since I found out he's missing. I just don't know. Greg doesn't know either."

"You've asked him?"

"I haven't. I just know."

"You just know that he doesn't know?" She smiled, and a small laugh broke the tension.

"Greg wouldn't hurt anybody. Not on purpose. And I think if he'd really shot the guy, he'd turn himself in."

"You think?"

James just looked at her.

His gaze unnerved her, and she looked away.

"See what I mean?" he said. "Sometimes knowing things isn't any fun. You of all people should know that. I'm not helping to send Caleb's dad to prison, especially when I don't even know what happened." He paused. Then, "So, what are you going to do?"

"Are you asking me if I'm going to help send Caleb's dad to prison?"

He didn't answer.

"Of course I don't want that, but we can't not tell the truth, James."

"I haven't lied to anyone. I told the police that I didn't see anything, and I didn't."

"You told them you heard the shot?"

"I did. I said I couldn't tell where it came from, and that's the truth. I couldn't." He took her hand. "How about we check out this crazy Nautikus theory of yours before you make a decision?"

"OK. You sure we can't go today?"

He laughed. "You'd be some sorry, 'bout time we got out into open water."

"Fine. So, why is my awesome theory so crazy?"

"Because no lobsterman would leave his boat behind."

"But you said his dad bought him that boat. Maybe he doesn't value it as much as you value yours."

She saw something in James's eyes in that moment that she hadn't seen there in weeks: hope.

Chapter 29

By Wednesday, Emily finally felt she was catching up on her sleep. And it was a good thing. Because her people were due to start arriving.

Her mom, sister, and sister's family were coming on the second ferry. They said they were coming to help, but Emily had her doubts. She just thought they wanted a few extra days on the island, and she couldn't imagine how much help her sister was going to be with a husband and two young kids in tow.

Nevertheless, she was thrilled that they were coming and got to the terminal twenty minutes before they were due to arrive. She couldn't even see the ferry yet, but she knew it was out there somewhere, on its way to her, with her family aboard.

Finally, the boat came into view, and she was practically bouncing on her feet. It was going to be *so great* to have some of *her people* here.

Her mother drove up the plank and off the ferry so slowly, she couldn't believe the ferry workers didn't holler at her. She wondered if she'd been that slow her first time. She doubted it. She'd told her mother that she didn't need to bring a vehicle, but she'd insisted. "Didn't want to be a burden."

Emily's mom's car pulled up in front of Emily, and the window rolled down. It was her sister driving, not her mom. "Hi, Meg!" Emily bent down to look into the car. "Mom? You OK?" She was sheet-white.

"No, I am not OK."

Meg looked at her. "She's a bit seasick."

Emily looked out at the sea. "Really? It's perfectly calm out there."

"Well, not calm enough!" her mother snapped.

Meg rolled her eyes.

"Why don't you park, and then get out and get your land-legs back."

"No," her mother said. "I just want to go lie down. Please take me to your house."

Emily stood up and blew out a puff of air. *This isn't starting out quite like I'd envisioned it.* "OK then, follow me."

Meg did follow her, so closely that Emily thought she was going to push her ahead with her bumper. Finally, they pulled into Emily's driveway, and three generations of Morse women spilled out of the car, followed by an elderly Basset hound.

"You brought Benjamin?" Emily said, trying to keep the horror out of her voice.

"Of course, but don't worry, we won't bring him to the wedding."

"But I don't know if your hosts want a dog in their house."

"Oh, that's OK. We can just kennel him at night if we have to. There must be a kennel nearby, right?"

It was so funny, Emily couldn't find it in herself not to laugh at her sister. A boarding kennel? *Oh sure, you can drop him off between your round of mini golf and your stop at the juice bar.*

Meg's two daughters began running circles around the car. "Finally, we're free!" One of them said.

Emily looked at Meg. "They stayed in the car for the whole ferry ride?"

"Yeah, Mom didn't want them to get out. Didn't think it was safe."

"Safe? Seriously, Mom? It's safer than a car."

"You can't drown in a car."

Actually, you could, but she didn't want to argue that point. "OK, well come on in."

"Are they OK out here?"

"Absolutely," Emily said, "safest place on earth."

"Yeah? That's not what we hear," her mom said.

"What? What are you talking about?" Had her mother heard about Kevin?

"We watch the news." She looked around Emily's home, the home she loved so much, the home she was so grateful for, the home she was actually sad about leaving. "This is awfully … *snug*."

"Yes, it is," Emily said defensively. "It's also free. And I love it."

"If you say so." She looked around. "Just not much room for your father and me."

"The couch is a foldout."

"A foldout? Your father can't sleep on a foldout! His hips!"

Emily took a deep breath. "Mom, what's wrong? Why are you acting like this?"

Meg put an arm around her mother. "Mom gets a little stressed out at weddings. She was like this at mine too."

"Stressed out? But everything's been done. You don't have anything to be stressed out about!"

"I'm not stressed out. I'm just seasick. Can you please pull this couch out so I can lie down?"

Wowsa, this is going to be fun.

Emily and Meg got her situated, and then Emily said, "Why don't I give you and the girls a tour of the island, so Mom can rest? Then I'll take you to your host's home."

Benjamin and the girls reluctantly piled into Emily's car. Emily wasn't thrilled to have a stinky, slobbery Basset hound in her backseat, even less thrilled when the dog put two front paws on the console beside her and began panting in her ear and drooling on her shoulder, but she didn't know what else to do with the old guy. She was sure glad Abe and Lily were believers, because it was going to take a good dose of Holy Spirit power to put up with Benjamin. Last she'd heard, his bladder was failing. *Boarding kennel—unreal.*

She took her family around the loop, and Meg was appropriately impressed, oohing and aahing at all the right times. She stopped at The Pizza Place and took them inside to introduce them to her wedding planner. Upon smelling baked cheese, both girls were starving.

Kim was as cordial as ever, didn't even blink at having to cook a whole veggie pizza to sell two slices, but when Meg went to show her daughter where the bathroom was, Kim whispered, "We have a problem."

Of course we do. "What?"

"Some of our hosts are backing out."

"What?" Emily cried. "Why?"

"They are PeeWee fans."

"PeeWee has fans?" Wonders never ceased.

"Apparently."

"I don't understand. What does PeeWee have to do with anything?"

"Duh. Some people think James is the bad guy in the Linville situation."

"They do?" Emily cried, too loudly.

"Shh. I don't think they think James killed anyone, but if PeeWee says James is a bad guy, then some people are going to follow his lead. But don't worry, I can take some guests, and I'll find places for the rest. You got any extra room?"

"Most definitely not. And James's guest room is taken too. I think it was empty when I originally volunteered it, but now it's got a sternman in it."

She nodded understandingly. "OK, give me time to sort it out, but just don't put anyone anywhere without verifying it's still a go."

Emily nodded as Meg returned. "After the girls eat, can you take me somewhere with sushi?"

"Sure," Emily said. "They serve it at the boarding kennel."

Chapter 30

Emily's father and Meg's husband arrived on Friday with some troubling news. Frank Bennett, who had been Emily's pastor her whole life, was sick and would not be able to make the wedding.

The wedding was tomorrow. They had no one to officiate.

"Isn't there a church on the island? A real one with a pastor?" her dad asked. He didn't even try to hide his disdain for Emily's house church.

"There is. And I've never met him."

"No time like the present," he said heartily, as if that were funny.

She dropped him off with her mother, and her brother-in-law off with Meg, and then ran to The Pizza Place. "My pastor's not coming!" She could practically feel her blood pressure rising.

"Don't panic," Kim said. "I'll ask Pastor Tim."

TRESPASS

The idea made Emily sick. "Isn't he going to be annoyed? A bunch of people decide the only church on the island, his church, isn't good enough, so they start their own, and it grows in leaps and bounds while his shrinks? Then one of them needs his help to get married?"

Kim bit her lower lip. "He's a follower of Jesus, right? So he won't think like that. He'll want to help."

Emily had her doubts, but she also had to go. Her father had forgotten his medication, and she had to go see if they had any at the clinic. (Her father couldn't *believe* they didn't have a pharmacy.)

They did have what she needed at the clinic, but couldn't dispense it without a prescription. Emily raced home, made her father call his doctor to get a copy of the prescription only to learn that he couldn't get a copy because that prescription had already been filled. Emily wrestled her father into the car—he kept insisting there had to be an easier way—and took him to the clinic to see the doctor, who examined him and prescribed him the medication he needed.

She didn't have time to get him back to her house before meeting the next ferry, which

Naomi and her family, along with more of Emily's family, were supposed to be on.

Naomi came screaming off the ferry, wearing a pair of brightly colored silk fisherman pants that looked like they'd come straight off a boat from Thailand. Emily hugged her best friend tightly, whispering in her ear, "Fisherman pants? How appropriate."

"I thought you'd appreciate that."

Emily saw her Uncle Simon and his wife Christine approaching, and let go of Naomi to hug them. Trailing behind them were her cousins Lydia and Israel, and Israel had brought his wife—Emily, in her panic, couldn't remember her name—and his two young children. *Why didn't we just go to Vegas? Why didn't we just go to Vegas?*

She'd just finished hugging the cousin-in-law with no name when she heard Uncle Bill's booming voice. "Where's the beautiful bride?" And suddenly Aunt Wendy had wrapped her in a perfumed embrace.

Emily saw that they'd brought three of her cousins along: Jacklyn, Jeremiah, and Jennesae, as well as Jennesae's husband, Carl. Oh boy. She thought they'd only RSVP'd for Jeremiah, and she only had one car. Oh well, at least they hadn't brought all five of their kids.

"Janice and Jacob will be on the next ferry," Uncle Bill boomed.

Oh boy for real. She had no idea where all these people were supposed to go; Kim was still making pizzas, and James was still fishing.

"You OK, sugar?" Naomi asked, squeezing her hand.

"Absolutely." Emily cleared her throat and raised her voice. "Hi, everybody. I'm so glad you all came! I'm not sure of the exact sleeping arrangements, but we'll get that worked out soon. In the meantime, I'm going to shuttle you to my fiancé's house. It's close by." *Everything's close by, Emily, it's an island.* "I mean, it's closer, and bigger, than my house. So, whoever wants to go first, climb into my car." She pointed. "And I'll be back for the rest of you in just a few minutes."

"What are we supposed to do in the meantime?" Aunt Wendy asked in horror. It appeared her makeup was melting off.

Emily looked at the ocean. "Enjoy the view? I'll be quick."

There was a brief squabble about the first trip. Her father refused to budge from his spot in the front seat. Carl needed to use a phone and was furious that he had no cell service. But he wouldn't go anywhere without

Jennesae, and Jennesae didn't want to leave Wendy for some reason. Naomi's family stepped back. "We can go last."

Emily shot her an "I love you" with her eyes.

Emily drove her loud guests to James's house, only *thinking* about smashing her head into the steering wheel when Carl asked if there was a killer on the loose and would they be staying somewhere safe.

When she opened the door to James's house, she found Lucas sitting on the couch. "What are you doing here?"

Lucas looked up at her assorted guests. "What are all *you* doing here?"

"We're not sure where people are staying yet, but they're just going to hang out here until I can talk to Kim, OK?"

"Sure, but where are you going?"

She still had one foot outside. "I've got more people waiting to be shuttled up here."

"Oh! I'll help."

He ran outside and jumped in his truck, a 1995 Ford that made more noise than God when he started it up. But dutifully, miraculously, he made trip after trip, back and forth to the ferry, and more than one of her cousins remarked at how friendly and charming he was. And Lydia said he was smoking hot. *Oh dear.*

TRESPASS

By the time the last ferryfull had been delivered, there was nowhere to sit, and barely anywhere left to stand in James's house. Thanks to Lucas, a few people had been delivered to their hosts, but most were still waiting for assignments. Emily was ready to have a nervous breakdown. James came through his front door, his hair on end, his clothes soaked in sweat, smelling of bait, and his eyes wide. Emily introduced him to everyone, and many of them took a step back.

"Why are you late?" Emily said through gritted teeth.

"My sternman quit on me today. I had to do it all myself. He is so fired."

Emily's eyes flashed fire at him. "Don't you dare!"

James's face screwed up in confusion, but he didn't have time to question her sudden allegiance to his wayward sternman.

"Go get in the shower. We've got rehearsal in twenty minutes."

Kim came through the door then and pulled her into the bathroom. "Pastor Tim is a no-go."

"What? Why?"

"He has other commitments."

"See? I told you." Emily put her head in her hands.

"Don't panic. I've got another idea. Absolutely anyone can get ordained online with the Global High Spirit Church and instantly be able to legally marry someone. Only costs fifty bucks." When Emily's face didn't immediately light up, Kim said, "I'll pay for it." Still no light, so Kim said, "I'll even do it. I'll become ordained. I'll marry you."

Emily finally laughed, but it was a weak offering. "I don't know. The Global High Spirit? Sounds like witchcraft." She thought for a second. "The bank!" she cried. "Don't all banks have notary publics?"

It was Kim's face's turn to fall.

"What? Our bank doesn't have one?"

"No, we do, but it's Jane Crockett."

"Perfect!" Emily cried.

"Seriously?"

"Yes, I love Jane! She probably doesn't believe in the social construct of marriage, but get her here! Get her daughter too. Right now, get them to the beach!"

Chapter 31

Lucas stayed behind to entertain the guests—Lydia was particularly excited about this—and James and Emily shuttled the necessary personnel to the rehearsal. They were just about to start when Emily realized she'd forgotten her parents, and raced across the island to retrieve them. She got to her house just in time to find Meg trying to mop up Bassett pee before Emily could find out. But Emily didn't have a single iota of energy to spare worrying about urine. "Come on, get in the car, we're late!"

Emily tore back to the beach, where a small crowd of locals had gathered to watch the affair. She saw several of her students and waved to them, trying to look like her cheery self, when inside she just wanted to die. *Why do people do weddings? Why?* What had she been thinking bringing all these people out here?

Jane climbed off her bicycle, and Emily turned to James.

"Yeah, I heard," he said without expression.

"Is it OK?"

"Oh sure, why not?"

Jane's dreadlocks were piled two feet atop her head; hence, no bike helmet, and she wore an elaborate array of colorful garments—but when it came to getting folks hitched, she was a pro. She kept the unwieldy group on task and moving right along, and soon, they were all headed to Abe's basement for dinner.

"What are all your other guests going to eat?" James mumbled as he piled his plate high with Lily's famous potato salad, which was almost more bacon than potato. Emily thought that might be what made it so famous.

"Lucas and Kim are on it. They're helping them get takeout."

"Takeout? You mean pizza?"

"No, a lot of them wanted seafood, so Kim and Lucas are going to fetch it for them from The Big Dipper."

"Oh. I hope your fifty cousins don't want lobster. The Big Dipper doesn't serve lobster."

"I don't have *fifty* cousins. I have seventeen. And thank God that they're not all here. Lucas is cooking lobsters on your stove for people who want them."

James looked aghast. "You're kidding." He took a giant bite of potato salad. "Maybe we should stay here tonight, in Abe's basement."

She tittered. "Can't. A bunch of my guests are staying here."

"Really? I thought Abe was only hosting Meg and her family."

"Well, we had some hosts back out—"

"Back out? Why, because of PeeWee?"

"Yes, because of PeeWee. I guess he has allies. But it doesn't matter, because Abe and Lily are taking on extras. So are you, by the way. Kim's been collecting air mattresses from all over the island."

"See?" James raised an eyebrow. "Things just get done around here. They just have a way of working out."

Unless you're from Nautikus. "Maybe." Emily was more prone to credit Kim's hustle than some sort of island magic. "But next time we do this, we are going to Vegas."

They stayed at Abe's house for as long as they could, but eventually, they had to return to reality—James's house.

There were lobster shells *everywhere*. Stacks upon stacks of butter-soaked paper plates. "You guys do know we're serving lobster tomorrow, right?" Emily asked.

Her cousin Nathan belched. At least she *thought* it was Nathan. She hadn't seen him in years. "No such thing as too much lob-stah," he slurred, his western Maine pronunciation rivaling any Downeast accent. He was holding a beer can, which he tipped up, realized was empty, and then threw on the floor. He looked at Lucas. "Any more?"

"You didn't tell me your family was a bunch of lushes," James said.

"Ah, the island brings it out of people," Lucas said, handing Nathan another beer. He looked at Emily. "Your family managed to buy every single microbrew on the island."

Emily didn't know what a microbrew was— Tiny beers? Tiny drunkenness?—but she nodded as if this was impressive.

Kim appeared, out of breath. "OK, everyone is fed, and everyone has a place to sleep."

Emily threw her arms around her. Kim tried to wriggle free, but Emily held on for as long as she could. "I don't know how I'll ever thank you. Without you, I would've died. Literally. Dead."

Kim laughed. "I didn't say they had *beds* to sleep in, but they all have a roof over their heads. There are ten people staying here."

"Ten?" James cried.

"But they all have air mattresses."

TRESPASS

"Good thing I'm on town water," James said.

"Don't think I didn't think of that. No one with a well has more than four guests. So, I think I'm done for the evening. I'll see you bright and early, OK?" she said to Emily.

Emily nodded.

"No, I mean *really* early. The stylist will be at your house at six, so your hair needs to be clean and dry by then."

"Six?" Emily was horrified.

"Beauty takes time." She gave Emily a kiss on the cheek. "See you in a few hours. Your wedding is going to be perfect."

Emily had never known perfect to be such a relative term.

Chapter 32

If Emily got any sleep at all the night before her wedding, she was unaware of it. Her father's snoring didn't help matters much, nor did her mother's frequent trips to the bathroom, for each of which she turned on every light in the house. She was *so glad* her mother had come early to help.

When the digital clock beside her bed read four o'clock, she gave up and flung the covers off. She was getting married today.

Right?

Right.

Right?

She had to see James. Yes, it was against the rules, and yes, she was being dramatic, but no, she didn't care. She was going to *make* him promise to turn Greg in. If they didn't find Kevin tomorrow, they *had* to tell the truth. She pulled on some clothes and snuck down the stairs, using her phone for a flashlight.

TRESPASS

She slowly opened the door, aware of the irony that she was *again* trying to sneak out on her parents. Old habits die hard and slowly.

"Where are you going?" her mom croaked. Old habits indeed.

"Nowhere. I'll be right back."

"You're not going to see James, are you?"

"Mom, you don't even believe in luck."

"I'm not talking about luck. I'm talking about propriety. About tradition."

Emily rolled her eyes in the dark.

Her dad sat up. "What's going on?"

"Emily's sneaking out."

"I'm not sneaking out, Mom. This is *my house*."

"Where's she going?" her dad asked.

Emily gave up then and simply walked out, closing the door behind her. Maybe they'd go back to sleep and think it had all been a dream.

The island was eerily still. No lights on in any houses. No headlights on the road. She realized she'd never driven around the island at four in the morning before.

James's house was as dark as the rest. She creaked the door open slowly, praying someone wasn't sleeping pressed up against it.

No one was, but she did have to step over someone to get to the stairs. Now what? She hadn't really thought this through. Was she going to creep into his bedroom and lay at the foot of his bed like Ruth? She'd thought he'd be up by now.

"What are you doing?" a raspy voice asked from behind, making her jump.

She turned to see Lucas sitting up on the floor.

"What are you doing down here?" she asked.

"He gave away my bedroom. And fired me. What are you doing here? What's wrong?"

She couldn't believe the amount of concern she heard in his voice. "Nothing's wrong. I just need to talk to James. And please don't tell me I'm not supposed to see him today. I know that."

He was extricating himself from a sleeping bag. "Hang on, I'll go get him."

Emily was hesitant.

Lucas read it on her face. "Don't worry. What's he going to do, fire me?"

"I told him not to fire you," Emily whispered.

"Will you guys keep it down?" someone said from the corner. She didn't recognize the voice.

"Sorry," Emily whispered as Lucas scaled the stairs. She watched him go, and then she stood there awkwardly, alone in the darkness. Well, technically she wasn't alone; she was in a room full of sleeping relatives. But she *felt* alone.

Lucas reappeared soon enough, with James behind him. James had obviously still been asleep. "What's wrong?" he asked.

"Can we talk?" she whispered.

He nodded, took her by the hand, and led her down the hallway to the bathroom. He pulled her in, shut the door behind them, and flicked on the small light over the mirror. Then he squinted at her. "What's up?"

"I'm sorry to wake you up, and I'm sorry to break the rules, and I'm not trying to be a drama queen, I swear—"

He put his hands on her upper arms and squeezed, scooching a little to look her in the eye. "Honey, what's up?"

"I just ... I'm kind of freaking out."

"About the Linville thing?"

"Yeah." A long breath rushed out of her. "About that. I really need you to promise that you're going to do the right thing. I mean, I hope we find good news tomorrow, but what if we don't? You *have* to tell someone."

He leaned back against the counter. "All this time, Em, I've been *trying* to do the right thing. Don't you know that?"

She knew no such thing. "I don't understand. You've been keeping a secret. You've been covering for someone."

He ran a hand over his face, and it made a scratching sound when he got to the stubble on his cheeks. "I think that my idea of the right thing and your idea of the right thing are two different things. What does it accomplish if I point the finger, when, I remind you, *I don't really know anything*? What does that do? Nothing. It just hurts more people."

Emily grew frustrated. "But what about God's right and wrong?"

James nodded thoughtfully. "I promise you, Em, I have prayed and prayed over this. And you know what I've heard in my spirit?"

Emily shook her head.

"That the people involved, *all* of them, will have to answer to God for everything they've done. It's not up to me to be the long arm of justice. God's got this."

"So you're not going to promise to tell the cops what you saw?"

"I'm sorry, I really don't like disappointing you, but no, I'm not going to tell anyone anything. I really don't have much to tell, Em."

"OK."

"OK?"

"Yeah," she said. "I'm going to go now."

"Who's Linville?" a now half-sober Nathan asked from behind the bathtub curtain, scaring the tar out of both of them. They laughed, and via telepathy, agreed not to answer him.

"We OK?" James asked.

"Yeah. I guess so. I've got to get my hair done now. I love you."

"Love you too. More than you know."

She slipped away, realizing she would probably never be able to *make* James do anything. And bizarrely, she loved him even more for it.

Chapter 33

Emily tentatively stepped into her dress, and Meg helped pull it up around her. She got the cap sleeves up over her shoulders, and Meg went behind her to zip up. Emily heard the zipping sound and sucked in her belly, but then the zipping sound stopped, and she still had quite a draft on her back. "What's wrong?"

"Um, just give me a sec." Meg pulled and yanked and twisted and then tried again.

"Is the zipper broken?" Emily felt her pulse speed up. She was also getting a headache. Probably from all the bobby pins. How many had the stylist used? She'd lost count. At least six hundred. Probably six hundred and sixty-six.

Meg was quiet. Too quiet. Emily knew what this meant. And she wasn't going to panic. She was just going to get emergency help. She went to the top of her stairs and hollered, "Kim!" as loudly as she could.

"Coming!"

TRESPASS

Kim ran up the spiral stairs and looked at her. "Oh dear."

"Yeah, so I've been doing some emotional eating lately."

"No worries. I'll call Mabel."

"The bossy woman from the power co-op?"

"The one and only. She's also a talented seamstress. Who do you think hemmed your dress?"

"Oh yeah." Emily had forgotten about that, how her dress had just "had" to come up a half an inch. Was it really going to matter when she was standing in sand?

"Well, that was nice of her. She doesn't even know me."

"I know. And she's a PeeWee fan too. I had to sweet talk her."

"Why does PeeWee have so many friends?"

"I dunno. Because his grandmother was friends with hers."

"Seriously?"

"Probably something like that. Now take the dress back off. I'll go call her."

Mabel arrived in minutes, and she was all business. She made Emily put the dress back on, and then fiddled with the fabric a bit before demanding she take it back off. Emily was exhausted, and it wasn't even noon yet.

She heard Kim downstairs, trying to give her mother directions so she could go get the cake. *I don't know if that's such a good idea, Kim.* She wasn't sure her mother could handle the pressure. No sooner had she had the thought that she heard Kim say, "Never mind. I'll just call Lucas."

Man, that guy is the best sternman ever.

By the time Emily finally got herself put together and headed toward the beach, she was starving, but she was also relieved. It seemed as though all the hard stuff had been done—most of it by Kim.

She looked amazing. Her makeup looked like that of a movie star. Her hair had never looked so good, in an elegant, tiara-embracing updo with a few large ringlets dancing around her shoulders. And her dress now fit like a glove, as if she'd never even had all that extra pizza. Mabel had even given her an extra half-inch—"dancing room," she'd called it. *I hate to break it to you, Mabel, but I'm marrying James Gagnon. I don't think there's going to be much dancing.*

The beach looked gorgeous, with its flower-covered arch and its neat rows of chairs. She wondered how many of those Lucas had set up. She noticed him standing toward the back, very close to Lydia. Maybe they weren't such a bad couple after all. Emily hoped Lydia liked to cook.

Jane was standing up front, looking rather presentable after all, with some sort of official I'm-qualified-to-marry-people sash around her neck. Sara sat alone in an empty row on Emily's side, with a floor-length black dress and a black sun hat. If it had been anyone else, Emily might have been offended by all the black, but she was just honored that Sara had even come—and that she'd worn a dress.

She saw James's truck then, and she watched him climb out of it. He was wearing a suit and tie. She knew he was uncomfortable; she knew he was too hot, but didn't he look amazing. The handsomest man she'd ever seen. Their eyes met, and the look he gave her made her knees weak. He looked smitten.

Brent, John, and James headed for the front, and most of the wanderers found seats. Thomas and his family sat in Sara's row. So Emily did have islanders on her side after all.

Some rubberneckers stood around the periphery. Again, she saw several students. Guess she hadn't needed to invite more islanders after all. They just showed up. She hoped they wouldn't also show up for the food afterward.

Chloe came along one side of her.

"You look amazing, kiddo."

"So do you, Coach."

Naomi came along the other side of her and handed her a bouquet. "I'm so, so happy for you, Emily. You deserve this fairytale. I'd hug you, but I don't want to mess up your makeup."

Emily laughed nervously.

"You ready?" Kim mouthed to her from twenty feet away.

She nodded and stepped over to her father, who looked surprised to see her there. She took his arm.

A young girl stepped up front with a flute. Emily recognized her from school, but didn't know her yet. She was still in the middle school wing. She was some distant cousin of James's, and Kim had said they needed a flutist, so there she was. When she began to play, Emily understood Kim's motivation. It was haunting and take-your-breath-away beautiful.

Kim nodded at Chloe, who began down the aisle. Emily caught Thomas watching her as she went, and his eyes overflowed with admiration.

Naomi began her march forward, and Emily's stomach twisted. She looked at James, who was gazing at her, and her stomach steadied. *We may not always agree, but that man will always be a rock.* This idea gave her tremendous comfort.

It was her turn. With trembling legs, she began to walk forward, which wasn't easy in her heels. She should have worn them to the rehearsal, she realized, but she made it to the front, kissed her dad on the cheek, and then took her man's hand. He squeezed it.

James had forbidden the practice of making up their own vows. He'd wanted something traditional, something, he said, that couldn't possibly result in embarrassment for him. So, they repeated their vows after Jane, and Emily didn't even really think about them as she spoke them. She was just so happy to be there, with him, in the sun, in front of the ocean. She was just so happy to be becoming his wife. And when he slid the ring on her finger, she thought her heart might burst right out of her chest.

"I now pronounce you husband and wife," Jane cried, and Emily was certain she heard true joy in Jane's voice. "You may kiss the bride."

James didn't just kiss her. He dipped her and planted his lips on hers as though he'd been waiting his whole life to do so. The crowd oohed and aahed so loudly, Emily was actually embarrassed, and pounded on his shoulder to let her up, which, several seconds later, he did.

She followed her bridesmaids down the aisle, and then Kim caught them. "Don't go anywhere! Back to the water for pictures!"

They obeyed, and spent the next hour and a half striking poses for a photographer Emily had never seen before but Kim said came highly recommended.

Finally, just when Emily was sure she was going to pass out from hunger, they were dismissed to join the reception, which was already in full swing. Much to Emily's surprise, it *didn't* smell like diesel inside the boat shop, and Kim (or some of her minions) had decorated it to look like the finest banquet hall.

James wasted no time. As soon as they'd been announced, he led her straight to the food, where she enthusiastically grabbed a lobster roll. So much for swearing off the lobster and sticking to the salad.

The cake looked as professional as any Emily had ever seen. Sally Trimble, whoever that was, had really outdone herself. For about a tenth of the normal cost.

At each place setting, Kim (or minions) had set a can of Moxie and a plastic champagne glass. And though Emily loved the cute idea, she didn't have time for a glass, and just drank half the can in one long haul. Then she dug into her lobster. She noticed James wasn't eating. He was just staring at her. "If you don't eat that, I will," she said.

He laughed. "Help yourself. I hate lobster. But, honey, you are so, so beautiful. I need you to know that."

Then, even though her mouth was full of lobster and she had mayo on her lips, she kissed him, and he kissed her back.

As she was winding down from her feasting, James leaned over to whisper into her ear, "Just so you know. I kicked everyone out of the house."

She raised an eyebrow. "You kicked my family out of your house?"

"I did." He smirked. "You're married to me now. I no longer need to be nice to your family. I've sent Brent around delivering the news. They need to get their stuff out by seven o'clock. They can either catch the last ferry or spend the night at your house.

"I'm not sure Lauren and Mike would appreciate that," Emily said, speaking of her landlords.

"Your mom will be there to keep everything a tight ship. Now, would you like to dance?" He stood up and held out a hand.

"Seriously?"

"I would never joke about such a thing."

"I thought you couldn't dance?"

"I've been watching YouTube how-to's."

She laughed, polished off her second Moxie, and took his hand.

They danced, and he absolutely *could* dance. She wondered if he'd been fibbing about his inability. After the song was over, she stopped and headed for the head table, but he grabbed her, pulled her back, and they danced some more.

They took a short break to cut the cake, and James fed her a bite as gently as possible, as if it had never occurred to him to smash cake into his bride's face. Which it probably hadn't.

Then they danced some more.

And sure enough, when they got to his house later, it was empty, still, and dark.

And James took her breath away when he picked her up and carried her over the threshold, into their home, into their new life.

Chapter 34

When Emily woke up on Sunday morning, she couldn't believe how happy she was. She looked around and saw that James was already up. She could smell coffee. Ah, so he *was* perfect. They didn't have time to dillydally on their first day as a married couple. Zachary Brown was going to be running the church service in their home, and they wanted to be long gone, on course for Nautikus, before the church folk started showing up.

Lucas had asked if he could still come to church. James had said of course—what else should he say to that?—and then said he could have another shot at sternman too if he wanted.

James looked up as she came into the kitchen. "Coffee's hot. I'm ready to go when you are."

She laughed. Why had she married a morning person? "How long have you been up?"

"Hours. Let's get going. I don't know how long we'll need to spend on Nautikus, and I don't want to be on the water after dark."

She grabbed her coffee and took it with her upstairs to get dressed.

The voyage was a gorgeous one, though she did get a little nervous when they got out onto the open water, and the boat started to pitch a bit as they headed into the wind, and the only land she could see was very, very far away. James, seeming to sense her unease, put his arm around her and pulled her close.

As Nautikus grew bigger through their windshield, Emily grew more nervous. Not because she was nervous to go there—she wasn't scared of the place, no matter what James told her—but because of what they might *not* find there.

Or maybe there *was* something about the place. Something dark. The closer they got, the more the giddiness she'd been riding high on for the last twenty-four hours seemed to dissipate. What *was* this place?

James cut the engine down to next to nothing, and they drifted into the almost-deserted public landing. The harbor was peppered with moorings, but there weren't nearly as many as there were in Piercehaven's harbor.

"How many people live here again?" Emily asked quietly even though there was no one around to overhear her. Still, she felt as though she was being watched.

"About two hundred year-round."

"And in the summer?"

"Not sure. Maybe 220?"

She snickered. "Guess they don't like summer people either, do they?"

"Not many fishing communities do." James tied his boat up to the dock, climbed out, and then reached back for Emily, who gratefully took his hand. "OK, this is your barbeque. Where do we start?"

"I don't know. I was just going to find someone and ask where the Linville family lives."

James shook his head.

"You got a better idea?"

"Yeah. What did Jesus say? Let's find a man of peace."

"How are we going to do that?"

"Not sure, but if God goes before us here, there will be one."

"We're not exactly approaching a mission field here, James."

"Oh, but aren't we?"

They walked by two men sitting in a pickup truck. They appeared to be doing nothing. Just sitting there. But they both stared at James and Emily as they walked by, as if they had never seen other humans before. It gave Emily the shivers.

"Look, I see a steeple," James said.

Under the circumstances, Emily found a steeple sighting to be remarkably good news.

They headed toward it, and, as God would have it, it was just opening its doors for a Sunday service.

"Did you plan this all along? Is this why you wanted to go on a Sunday?"

"Nope, it never occurred to me till I saw the doors were open, but pretty slick, huh?"

"I doubt he's a churchgoer."

"I never said he was. Let's go."

An elderly usher greeted them at the door with a giant grin. "Good morning! Welcome, welcome! Come right in."

They entered the dimly lit sanctuary, and Emily looked around. "Wow, this is gorgeous."

"Yeah, I think this place has been around for a while."

They settled into a back pew and watched people walk in. None of the attendees appeared to be younger than seventy-five. An organ began to play, and a middle-aged woman with big hair entered through a door in the front. She carried a big, well-worn Bible and was obviously in charge.

"Or a *woman* of peace," Emily muttered.

James smiled. "That works too."

"Good morning!" the woman's voice sang out. "Isn't it a gorgeous day to worship the Lord?"

The music was dirgelike, but the sermon was lively, and, in Emily's estimation, spot on. Three different people invited them downstairs for coffee after the service, and they were heading that way when the pastor cut them off. "Welcome," she said, offering her hand, "I'm Pastor Patty. So glad to have you with us today."

They shook hands and exchanged names, and then Patty asked, point-blank, "What brings you to us this morning?"

James flinched.

"We're looking for someone," Emily said, though she could sense James willing her not to say too much. "Kevin Linville?"

"Oh?" Patty's face betrayed nothing. "And why are you looking for Kevin?"

Not "We're all looking for Kevin" or "Why are you looking for him here?" but "Why are you looking for Kevin?" Only someone who knew he wasn't really missing would ask that question.

James had apparently swallowed his tongue. "It's kind of a long story," Emily said, "but, well, there are people who are worried about him, and I just wanted to make sure he was OK so I could tell them that he is … OK." She stopped herself from saying "that he is *alive*."

"*Worried* about him? Why would they be worried about him?"

Emily understood then. She understood everything. Revelation flooded over her, and the relief was overwhelming. Kevin Linville was alive all right, alive and scared. And this woman was protecting him. "Pastor, we would *never* hurt anyone. We would never bring anyone harm. I don't think there's anyone left on Piercehaven who wants to harm Kevin, but even if there is, we won't tell them where he is. We just want to tell those who do care that he's all right."

"And why did these people send you? If they care so much, why didn't they come themselves?"

Emily paused. She didn't know the answer to that. She silently asked God for words, and they came immediately: "I'm sort of the type to stick my nose into others' business and try to problem solve."

Patty laughed at this, a genuine laugh straight from the gut. "Ah, I see. Isn't that one of the spiritual gifts? So if I tell you that Kevin is just fine, is that enough? Or do you need to see him?"

Emily was about to say, "It's enough," when James finally spoke. "I need to see him."

Patty raised a well-groomed eyebrow.

"I believe you," James said, "but I want to be able to tell people back home that I saw for myself."

"All right. OK if I come with you?"

James nodded quickly. "Of course."

"Excellent. Why don't you join me and the others for refreshments, and then I'll take you to him."

"You know *exactly* where he is?" Emily asked.

Patty smiled. "I keep pretty good tabs on my sheep."

So that's how Emily ended up doing dishes, her arms elbow deep in suds, wondering how just a few old people could dirty so many brownie plates. Finally, with everything scrubbed, she dried off to follow her husband and their new friend outside.

"That was the longest coffee hour of my life," James muttered to her.

Emily expected Patty to head toward a car, but she just walked down the street. "That's my house there," she said, pointing, "in case you ever need anything. Though you probably won't be back, will you?"

They didn't answer her.

"Yeah," she said softly, as if musing to herself, "Nautikus is an odd place. Not really into attracting visitors." They met someone on the street who went out of their way to pretend the three of them weren't there. "People like to ignore me. Until there's a crisis. Then I'm pretty popular." They walked by a "General Store" that looked like something off a dystopian movie set. Emily couldn't imagine trying to buy anything fresh there. Nautikus folks must be into gardening. She vowed to never complain about Marget's selection, or lack thereof, again.

Patty turned onto a small, narrow side street and Emily wondered if this was all a ruse, if she was just taking them into the woods to murder them. Then they stopped in front of a run-down trailer. Patty approached and knocked softly on the door. At first, there was nothing, and Emily was about to ask her to bang a little harder, but then the door opened, and a young, thin, nondescript young man stood in the opening.

"Hi, Kevin," Patty said. "Got a minute?"

Chapter 35

They stood in Kevin's living room, looking down at him. He had returned to his position in front of the television. A zombie video game was paused on the screen. Kevin looked longingly at it.

"Do you know these people, Kevin?"

He shook his head sheepishly.

Emily didn't know whether to hug him or slap him. She was certain she'd never felt so relieved, and when Kevin had opened that door, she had felt about a ton of tension leave James's shoulders. She was certain that years had just been added back onto his life.

"I'm James Gagnon. Remember me?"

James hadn't needed to ask that question. It was obvious Kevin knew who he was. He looked terrified.

"We're not here to hurt you, Kevin," James said. "If we were, we wouldn't have brought your pastor along."

He snorted. "My pastor? That's my aunt."

Of course she is.

"Either way, we mean you no harm, but do you have *any idea* what you've done?"

Kevin began to stammer. "I ... I ... I ... was just fishin'. PeeWee told me I could!"

"Not that," James said quickly. "I don't care about that."

You don't? Since when? But she let him talk.

"Do you realize that I thought you were dead? And the man who fired the gun? He thinks he killed you!"

"Yeah, well, he *tried* to kill me. So let him think it." He reached for a pack of cigarettes that were resting on an upside-down milk crate beside him. Patty quickly swatted them out of his hand. "Hey!" he cried.

"But he *didn't* kill you, and I don't even think he was trying to. I think he was just trying to scare you. What happened? Where'd you go?"

"What's it to you?"

Emily looked at James and saw that some of his relief was giving way to a fresh anger.

"Just answer the question, Kevin," Patty said calmly but firmly. "Because their version of events isn't sounding quite the same as the one you told me."

"I just left, man," Kevin said. Then he swore, and Patty glared at him. "Sorry," he mumbled.

"I just left," he said again, staring at the television.

"And you just left your boat floating there? Are you crazy?" James said.

"You left your father's boat?" Patty asked. There was a new chill to her voice. "Why would you do that, Kevin? *How* could you do that?" She looked at James. "He told me you people sank it."

James pinched the bridge of his nose as if in physical pain. "No, we didn't sink it. It drifted up on some rocks. PeeWee has since driven it back to its mooring. Kevin can go get it anytime ... or better yet, he can send someone else to get it."

Patty looked furious. But then she closed her eyes, and said, "Ah, I get it. You *wanted* them to think that you were dead."

"Well yeah," he sputtered, "so they didn't come finish the job."

"So you were just going to hide out here for the rest of your life?" James said.

Kevin didn't answer.

"How'd you get back here?"

Again, no answer from Kevin.

"His girlfriend brought him back at night," Patty said, staring at Kevin with a sad look on her face. "But I don't think many people know that. I don't even think her father does, unless she's told him since. I doubt he would have let her come all this way at night with his boat." Patty looked at James. "Do you have what you came for?"

"We do," James said. He held his hand out. "I don't know how we can thank you. You have no idea the lives you've helped."

She took his hand. "Can you find your way back?"

"Absolutely." James turned to go, and Emily followed him, but then abruptly, he turned back. "Did the Marine Police come looking for him? Or anyone official?"

Patty nodded. "Yeah, that was before I got involved. Someone met them at the dock, said they hadn't seen him. I don't know if they were lying or if they just didn't want the Marine Police here. Sorry about that. All this time, I really thought he was in danger."

James gave Kevin Linville one last look. "Did you ever really fear for your life, or were you just trying to have the last word?"

Kevin didn't answer.

Chapter 36

James walked so fast back to the public landing, Emily struggled to keep up with his long legs. She had a renewed compassion for her sister's stubby-legged Basset hound.

"Sorry," he said, when she started breathing hard, "just in a hurry to get back."

"I know. It's OK. I wish we could just call him."

"I don't want to take the time to look for a landline. If it weren't Sunday, I could hail him on the radio. But I think we're just going to have to hurry back and deliver the news in person."

"I can't believe it," Emily said. "I just can't believe it."

"*You* can't believe it? This was your idea! I never thought he'd be here, just sitting around wasting time." James jumped into his boat and then reached for her. "I didn't think my opinion of him could get any lower, but it has. I really hope I never see that guy again. Sorry, Father, but it's true. And I can't believe I'm saying this"—he started the engine—"but Harley Hopkins deserves better than that. She's the one who just dodged a bullet."

"Maybe she figured it out. Maybe that's why she snuck him off her island under the cover of darkness. She wanted to get rid of him."

"That's entirely possible. Anyway, let's talk about something else."

But they didn't. Not really. It was a long, slow, quiet trip back. Emily could see a difference in James's posture. His shoulders looked more relaxed; his jaw was less tight. She was so happy that this whole thing was over. Or *almost* over.

James came into Piercehaven Harbor hot, but there was no one around to wave angrily at him. He tied the boat to his mooring and then leapt into his launch. Soon he was rowing hard toward the landing.

And then they were in the truck, and it felt as though every minute was stretching into an unendurable hour. They got behind a Better Choice fuel truck, and James groaned.

"I've always wondered," Emily said. "Isn't Better Choice the only fuel company on the island? So what are they better than?"

"The company they put out of business ten years ago." He swerved across the yellow lane as if he was going to pass the truck.

Emily put a hand on the dashboard. "Don't do it, James. We're almost there. If we die now, someone else will have to go to Nautikus."

"I know, I know, but Greg doesn't deserve to go another second thinking he killed a man."

And then they were pulling into the driveway, and then James was running to the door. Then knocking impatiently.

Kim opened the door. "What are you two—"

"Can we come in?" James asked.

"Of course, James, what's wrong?" She looked at Emily for an answer, but Emily had no words. She tried to give her a reassuring smile as she walked by her into the house.

By the time Emily caught up with James, he was kneeling on the floor in front of Greg, as if he was about to propose marriage.

"What do you mean, he's alive?" Greg's eyes were wide, his mouth open.

"I mean we just saw him." James looked over his shoulder at Emily, and there was triumph in his eyes. "Tell him, Em."

"It's true, Greg. We just left him. He's alive and well. Well, as *well* as that guy can be, anyway."

James laughed with levity. "Oh yeah, the guy is a piece of work, but that doesn't matter. He's alive, Greg."

And then Greg's eyes filled with tears. "Oh, thank God. I really wasn't trying to hurt anyone," he said, so quietly that Emily almost couldn't hear him.

"Dad?" Caleb had appeared in a doorway. "What's going on? What's wrong?"

Emily looked at Kim, who looked just as confused as her son.

"Nothing's wrong, guys," Emily said. "Sorry, didn't mean to freak you out. We just knew that your dad was really worried about Kevin Linville, so we wanted to tell him that Kevin's been found, and he's OK."

Caleb didn't look satiated. "Why were you worried about that guy, Dad?"

"Because that's the kind of man your dad is," Emily said. "He cares about people." She didn't know how true this was, but she thought it was a good thing for Caleb to hear.

Kim crossed the room then and sat beside her husband. She put an arm around him and rested her head on his shoulder. Then she reached up and kissed him on the cheek. Her eyes said that she knew there was much more to the story, but that kiss said that she wasn't going to ask, at least not right now.

"I can't believe it," Greg said softly. "I just can't believe it."

Emily touched James on the shoulder. "We should go, honey. Let them get back to their evening. We've got others to tell, anyway."

James stood. "Right. OK, good night, guys. Sleep well."

"Oh, I will," Greg said and laughed. "Thank you, guys. I mean it."

"You're welcome," James said. At the door, he said to Emily, "Who else do we have to tell?"

"We have to tell Marine Patrol, don't we? And shouldn't we tell PeeWee? Not about Harley's late night run, but just that the guy is alive?"

James groaned. "Fine. But you can tell him, and we can do that one by phone."

Emily was horrified. "I don't want to talk to him! You call him!"

James laughed. "Fine, I'll call him. I told him never to talk to you again anyway."

They were just climbing into the truck when Kim opened the door and looked out at them. "Thank you, guys."

"You're very welcome," James said, his voice almost singsong.

"What were you guys doing on Nautikus, anyway?"

James looked at Emily and then gave Kim a big smile. "We were on our honeymoon."

***

Large Print Books by Robin Merrill

Shelter Trilogy
Shelter
Daniel
Revival

Piercehaven Trilogy
Piercehaven
Windmills
Trespass

Wing and a Prayer Mysteries
The Whistle Blower
The Showstopper
The Pinch Runner

Gertrude, Gumshoe Cozy Mystery Series
Introducing Gertrude, Gumshoe
Gertrude, Gumshoe: Murder at Goodwill
Gertrude, Gumshoe and the VardSale Villain
Gertrude, Gumshoe: Slam Is Murder
Gertrude, Gumshoe: Gunslinger City
Gertrude, Gumshoe and the Clearwater Curse

Robin Merrill also writes sweet romance as Penelope Spark:
The Billionaire's Cure
The Billionaire's Secret Shoes
The Billionaire's Blizzard
The Billionaire's Chauffeuress
The Billionaire's Christmas